THE RIDDLE OF THE FIGUREHEAD

By Rosalie Fry

THE RIDDLE OF THE FIGUREHEAD
THE ECHO SONG
THE MOUNTAIN DOOR
FLY HOME, COLOMBINA
SECRET OF THE RON MOR SKERRY
MATELOT, LITTLE SAILOR OF BRITTANY
A BELL FOR RINGELBLUME
THE WIND CALL
PIPKIN SEES THE WORLD

The Riddle of the Figurehead

WRITTEN AND ILLUSTRATED BY

Rosalie Fry

NEW YORK: *E. P. Dutton & Co., Inc.*

FIRST EDITION

Library of Congress Catalog Card Number: 63-8596

THE RIDDLE OF THE FIGUREHEAD

Chapter 1

SNAPDRAGON, moon daisy, love-in-a-mist, bachelor's buttons and Solomon's-seal; as she stooped over the garden border Stella wondered if the French gave their flowers such imaginative names—she would have to ask Marie-Thérèse when she arrived this evening. She picked one more crimson snapdragon, and some dark sprigs of scented rosemary, then turned and made her way slowly towards the house, trying to decide whether the flowers would look best on the spare-room chest of drawers or on the bedside table.

She was so busy with her own thoughts that she never so much as glanced towards the garden shed in which her brothers were busy building a sailing dinghy. But as she crossed the lawn, Peter spotted her and shouted, "Hi—Stella! Come and give us a hand, will you?"

Stella stopped in surprise; it wasn't often that the others wanted her help, or indeed included her in the boat-building work at all, in spite of the fact that the kit had been a joint gift to the three of them. When it had first arrived, at the start of the Easter holidays, she had been as keen as her brothers to begin the exciting job of assembly. But she soon discovered that building a boat was a long, exacting business over which the boys, especially Peter, were painstakingly slow and thorough—so thorough that there were moments when even thirteen-year-old Robert wondered secretly if they would really get the boat finished and afloat before the end of the summer. But he kept these doubts from his elder brother.

Stella, however, soon got bored with the detailed work and asked so many questions that her brothers became impatient, and this led to arguments and quarrels. After a while she began to avoid the shed, and as the weeks went by the boys came to look on the boat as theirs entirely, and even Stella herself almost forgot that she really had a share in it as well.

Now it was holiday time again and the long hours of daylight made it possible for the boys to work on the boat from dawn till bedtime, and Stella seldom saw them except at meals. This made Peter's call all the more surprising. She dumped her flowers hurriedly into the bird bath to keep them fresh, and ran across to the shed to see why she was wanted.

She found everything looking impressively workmanlike: large building plans were pinned to the walls while smaller sheets lay spread out over the workbench, their curling edges weighted with heavy tools and clamps. In the middle of the floor stood the boat herself, still upside down, but with panels and keel in place at last. Stella turned to her elder brother with a new respect.

"Oh, Pete, you've really made all those pieces into a boat after all!" she exclaimed, putting out a hand to stroke the curving hull. "What do you want me to do?" she added, only too anxious to help now that the boat was beginning to look so exciting.

"We've got to turn her right side up," said Peter. "I can manage this side if you'll go round with Robert. Now then, are you ready? O.K.—over she goes!"

When the boat stood right side up, she looked better than ever, although there were still a number of jobs to be completed.

"We must cut off the ends of those frames for a start, you'd better do that," said Peter, handing a saw to Robert. He himself moved across to the bench to pore over the plans and decide what to tackle next.

Stella stood for a moment watching a little forlornly, then, realizing that her moment of usefulness was over, and she herself no longer needed, she wandered out to the garden again, her trailing footsteps muffled by the sawdust on the floor.

Collecting her flowers from the bird bath, she made her way round to the kitchen where she found her mother busy making apricot jam. The only sounds to be heard in the quiet room were the bub-bub-bubble of the jam on the stove and the frantic buzzing of a single wasp, as it zoomed to and fro, trying to locate the source of the sweet, intoxicating smell.

"Oh, what a heavenly collection!" exclaimed Mrs. Bevan, smiling at the sight of Stella's bunch. "Would you like my yellow pottery jar? Flowers always look well in that."

Stella loved arranging flowers, and having filled the yellow jar at the sink, she went across to the window sill, where she was soon as deeply absorbed as her brothers outside in the shed. Mrs. Bevan smiled across at the bent dark head, glad of the temporary lull, for the boat had caused a good deal of squabbling, and so far the holidays had been anything but peaceful.

At last the final sprig of rosemary was satisfactorily arranged and Stella stepped back to admire the result of her work. Nothing remained but a handful of scattered leaves and stalks to be tidied away. Postponing this unattractive job she swept her muddles to one side, and leaning her elbows on the window sill, gazed out across the garden, to the roofs and chimneys of the little village that straggled down the hillside. At the foot of the hill a long line of sand dunes broke the force of the sea winds, protecting the village from the worst of the wild southwesterly gales that swept in from the sea at times. Beyond the dunes lay the golden sweep of a sandy beach, its wide arc culminating in a curious rocky promontory that curved out into the sea from the foot of the headland that bounded the western end of the bay. This promontory, known as Long Holm, was cut off from the headland at high water, the highest tides dividing it again into three separate islets. But the tide was low this morning and the rocks formed a mere continuation of the beach.

It was one of the still, hazy days that Stella loved, with the Devon coast spread like a low-lying cloudbank on the far side of the Bristol Channel, while the distant island of Lundy appeared as no more than a blur on the horizon. The soothing drone of muffled foghorns added their own weird enchantment to the tranquillity of the morning.

But the spell was abruptly shattered when the door flew open and Robert burst into the kitchen. With him came two more wasps.

"Phew! It's absolutely stifling in here!" he said disapprovingly.

"Well, either come in or stay out, but shut that door for goodness' sake!" exclaimed his mother, waving away the wasps.

"Shut it? But Mum, it's simply stewing in here!"

Mrs. Bevan sighed; she was hot and busy and in no mood for arguments.

"Can't you see I'm making jam?" she said wearily. "I'd far rather be hot than have half the wasps in Wales trying to commit suicide over the stove. What do you want in here anyway?"

Robert began to realise that he was not particularly welcome.

"Pete wants a kettle of boiling water," he said meekly.

Stella swung round and cried accusingly, "Boiling water? I thought you were supposed to be working on the boat!"

"If you'd troubled to learn the first thing about boat-building you'd know that plywood sometimes needs to be softened with boiling water to make it pliable," he retorted scathingly.

Stella changed the subject hastily.

"Look, Mum!" she said, holding up her jar of flowers. "Aren't these nice for Marie-Thérèse's room?"

Robert snorted.

"I'm getting absolutely sick of your precious Marie-Thérèse," he grumbled.

"How can you be sick of a person when you can't even remember what she looks like?" demanded Stella hotly.

"I remember enough to know she isn't worth all this fantastic fuss," he assured her.

"Oh, will you children stop wrangling, or else go and squabble outside!" cried their mother in exasperation. As a matter of fact she was growing very tired of Marie-Thérèse herself, since Stella could think and talk of nothing but the coming visitor. But she kept this feeling strictly to herself, determined that the visit should be a success, since Stella would be going to stay with Marie-Thérèse next summer.

Last year the boys had gone to Brittany to stay with a French family, on the understanding that Philippe, the son of the family, should pay a return visit this summer. But now Madame Griveau had written to say that her son Philippe had made friends with an English boy at school, and as a result had made such progress with his spoken English that she and her husband did not feel he was really in need of further conversational practice. And so they asked whether they might send their daughter Marie-Thérèse in his place.

Mrs. Bevan had seized upon the suggestion at once, feeling that it would be much easier for Stella to go next year if she already knew the daughter of the family. The boys had grumbled at first, but were soon too absorbed in boat-building to worry about much else. As for Stella, she began counting the days until Marie-Thérèse's arrival, and Robert's taunts were almost more than she could bear. Although he said nothing more for the moment something in his expression maddened her, so that she snatched up her flowers and rushed from the room, slamming the door behind her.

"Oh, Robbie, I do wish you wouldn't tease her so," pleaded Mrs. Bevan.

"But, Mum, she's so infuriating!" exploded Robert. "On and on and on about this beastly Marie-Thérèse."

"I know," agreed his mother, "all the same, she's had a pretty thin time these holidays, you know."

Robert felt uncomfortable, and because of this he spoke aggressively.

"Well the boat's hers as much as ours," he pointed out, "and it's got to be built before it can be sailed. I don't see that it's our fault if she's not interested in helping."

"Don't forget she's a good deal younger than you and Peter," his mother reminded him. "You two are old enough to enjoy a job of work, but at eleven one often prefers to play."

"She's more like a kid of ten, really she is!" exploded Robert. "I only hope Marie-Thérèse prefers playing, too, that's all. She must be getting on for fifteen, you know."

Mrs. Bevan sighed, wondering why her children were such firebrands, while she herself liked nothing so much as peace and quiet.

A hesitant tap sounded on the outside door. Mrs. Bevan went to open it.

"Why, Sammy!" she said gently, "what have you got there? Come in a minute while I shut the door, I'm trying to keep the wasps away from my jam."

A strange figure shambled into the room with a basket in his hand. Although his hair was thin and grizzled, it was impossible to guess whether he was an old man or a young one, since his slow, vacant smile showed that he was just a little simple. However, he was clever enough to have found and picked the mushrooms, which he now held out with pride.

"Oh, Sammy, what beauties!" Mrs. Bevan exclaimed. "I must certainly buy a couple of pounds of these." And with a laughing glance at Robert she added teasingly, "Marie-Thérèse is sure to like mushrooms!"

Robert grinned in reply.

"I don't know about that," he said. "We mostly lived on shellfish in their house, and pretty queer stuff some of it was too, I can tell you—I sometimes used to wonder if it was even cooked."

Mrs. Bevan brought her scales to the table, where Sammy insisted on selecting her mushrooms himself, allowing her only his choicest specimens, since she was one of his favourite customers.

When they had weighed out a couple of pounds, Mrs. Bevan calculated the price and fetched the money-jar from the dresser. Sammy was clever enough to find stuff to sell when he wanted to buy liquorice candy or ice cream, but the money itself was a complete mystery as far as he was concerned. So it was left to his customers to weigh his wares themselves and give him the correct price. And, since Sammy was a well-loved local character, he was often given more than his due, and certainly never less.

"And how's Aunt Martha today?" inquired Mrs. Bevan, for although Sammy himself seemed ageless, the old aunt with whom he lived grew frailer every year.

"She's so-so," replied Sammy indifferently. "But Willie's top-

top—look!" and plunging his hand into his pocket he brought out a long-tailed field mouse and set it down on the rim of the basket. It promptly ran up the handle and sat on the top, testing the air with quivering nose, one small forepaw raised enquiringly.

Mrs. Bevan wasn't awfully keen on mice, but she was getting used to Willie, who spent a good deal of time in Sammy's pocket, feasting on nuts and biscuit crumbs and any other delicacies that came his way. He was a plump little fellow with sleek brown fur, very different from the half-drowned object Sammy had rescued months ago from a water barrel. And because kind, simple Sammy had an extraordinary power over animals, Willie had never attempted to run away, choosing to remain in the shore cottage and become another of the assorted collection of livestock known throughout the village as "Sammy's creatures." Now, satisfied that there was nothing of any particular interest in or around the basket, he scuttled back by way of Sammy's sleeve and slipped down into the sagging pocket to continue his interrupted meal.

Sammy had no sooner left than there was a shout from the shed where Peter was still working on the boat.

"Hey! Robert!" he called, "isn't that kettle boiling yet?"

Before there was time for any reply he strode into the kitchen himself, grumbling under his breath. Catching sight of Robert sitting on a corner of the table he exploded, "Well, of all the useless, lazy—"

His mother cut him short.

"Now, look here," she interrupted, "I'm busy and I've had enough distractions this morning already. For goodness' sake, take your kettle and go, both of you. Oh, Stella, what on earth have you come back for?" She sighed, as yet another face appeared in the doorway.

"I only came to see what Sammy brought—oh I say, aren't they gorgeous, will we be having them for supper?"

This question gave her mother an idea, and instead of answering she asked unexpectedly, "Tell me, what is the tide doing?"

"Going out, lowish by now I should imagine—yes, look at the Holm," said Peter, crossing to the window. "But why do you want to know?"

"I was thinking of Marie-Thérèse," she replied in an innocent tone. "It occurs to me that people who like shellfish might very well like laverbread. Did you boys have laverbread in Brittany?"

"Can't say I remember it, but what's it matter, anyway? Even if Marie-Thérèse doesn't like it, we all do, so let's go and get some anyway!" said Robert with enthusiasm.

"Oh, no you don't!" cried Peter firmly, "you've been away long enough as it is. I can't spare you to go gallivanting off after laverbread just when we've got those rubbing beads to fix."

"There's no need for you all to go. Stella can quite well go on her own, especially as we really want it for Marie-Thérèse in any case," said Mrs. Bevan, determined to get her kitchen empty somehow. She was a tiny woman, not quite five feet tall, and even Stella topped her by a quarter of an inch, while the boys towered above her like giants. She was a quiet little person too, and often felt rather overwhelmed by her family. As a result she was sometimes inclined to give in for the sake of peace. However, she succeeded in clearing her kitchen now, as Peter swept Robert out to the boatshed and Stella ran off to fetch the tattered canvas bag they always used for laverbread.

"And change out of that skirt—it's much too good for the beach," her mother called after her.

Chapter 2

THE road that passed the Bevans' gate entered the village as a fine tarred highway, but once beyond the village it quickly dwindled to a rutted track that went wandering through the sand dunes to the shore. Stella followed this track, and was soon making her way across the wet sand towards the Long Holm promontory where small waves turned and sparkled along the edge of the rocks.

Before reaching the promontory, however, she turned aside in order to pass close to the shore cottage in which Sammy lived with his old Aunt Martha. The tiny cream-washed building crouched under the sheltering headland, its solid surrounding wall standing on the extreme edge of the sand. Shells lay at the base of this wall, and a tangle of drying bladder wrack left by an earlier tide, and already a-patter with sandhoppers. Leaning out from the wall of the cottage itself was a large wooden figurehead, all that remained of the *Evelyn Starr*, the little trading schooner of which Sammy's father had been skipper.

It was, in fact, this figurehead that had saved the skipper's life. He had been sailing home up the Bristol Channel years ago when his little, old ship had been overwhelmed by a tremendous gale. After a long and gallant struggle she was eventually driven ashore and battered to pieces on the rocks. Her skipper refused to leave her until she began to disintegrate around him, and he found himself floundering in the heavy sea, surrounded by floating wreckage. He often used to say that he would undoubtedly have been drowned if he had not caught sight of the familiar face of the figurehead rolling in the swell beside him. Using the last spurt of his ebbing strength he struggled through the waves towards her, and later, when the lifeboat picked him up, his arms were still clasped tightly round her painted neck.

There had been a time, long ago, when Stella had been a little afraid of the tall white-robed woman with her strange, hard-featured face and wild, unseeing eyes. But through the years this feeling had gradually given place to one of pity for the disconsolate, shorebound creature whose back-flung head was always turned so yearningly towards the sea that she would never sail again. Added to this was the friendly similarity of their names, for she had been told that her own name, Stella, meant "Star," which gave her a feeling of kinship with *Evelyn Starr*.

But today as she leant against the wall she stared up at the carved face as though seeing it for the first time, trying to imagine how it would appear to a newcomer such as Marie-Thérèse. There was no doubt about it, poor *Evelyn Starr* was extraordinarily plain. And yet by all accounts, old Captain Walters had thought her beautiful, repainting her with loving, if inartistic, care every year until his death. But there was nobody to paint her now, and year by year her fading colours mellowed in the sunshine, while the sea winds blurred and softened the salt-encrusted features. As a result much of the harshness was smoothed away and a gentler *Evelyn Starr* was gradually emerging, like a wistful shadow of her former rugged self. Perhaps Marie-Thérèse wouldn't think her so very hideous after all.

Sammy was not back from the village yet, but several of his creatures were about the place: Cawdaw, the one-legged jackdaw, was sitting on the roof, while a robin was sharing a crust of bread with a hedgehog on the doorstep. On the bench beneath the figurehead a sick hen dozed in a cardboard box. There was no sign of old Martha although the mingled smells of burning cork and wood smoke suggested that she was inside. Stella called out "good morning," as she always did when passing. There was no reply, nor did she expect one, for the old woman was something of a recluse and seldom seen outside her cottage. And yet it was well known that she herself saw everyone who passed from behind the dingy curtains that screened her tiny windows.

Stella suddenly remembered that she had come for laverbread, and with a final smile at *Evelyn Starr* she turned her steps towards the rocks where this oddly-named seaweed was to be found.

It was slimy-looking stuff, draping the wet rocks in greenish-black festoons. But where the tide had ebbed sufficiently to allow the weed to dry, it lay flattened against the rocks in crisp black layers. Stella peeled these off with a tearing sound, dropping them into her canvas bag as she followed the receding tide, until eventually she found herself pulling slippery streamers of dripping weed from rocks that were still surrounded by the sea.

There was a wonderful atmosphere of peace about this place, especially when the tide was low as it was this morning. Small waves lapped in without a sound and the distant drone of the foghorns was muted to a sigh. Far more insistent were the curious watery rustlings made by innumerable living organisms that covered the newly exposed rocks. Stella hummed contentedly under her breath, feeling herself in a world of her own, curiously remote from the world of humankind.

When she had picked all the laverbread she wanted she

looked around for a suitable rock pool, and finding one well clear of sand she turned her bag upside down, emptying the seaweed into the rocky basin. Here she washed it carefully, picking off diminutive mussels and scraps of shell, and weeding out the brilliant ribbons of inedible weed that grew entangled in the darker laverbread. Finally she swished the whole gleaming mass to and fro in the water, rinsing away the worst of the sand. It would all have to be washed again at home, of course, passing through many rinses of fresh water before it was entirely free of sand and grit and ready to be cooked.

With a final swirl she scooped up the dripping bundle, and dropping it into the canvas bag, she turned for home.

Stella was skirting the rocks, when she pulled up short, suddenly aware that she was being watched. She glanced into a miniature cove to her left and there, sitting upright on the sand, was a dark-coloured bird some eighteen inches tall. He was watching her warily, but to her surprise he did not move when she took a step towards him. Then she saw the reason; the poor bird was so heavily coated with thick black oil that even his front, which should have been white, was stained a dingy brown. It was hard to recognise this bedraggled object as the guillemot he was. The boys had found such birds before, and Peter had got a booklet from the R.S.P.C.A. giving instructions on how to treat these unhappy victims of oil pollution, many of them coated in waste discharged from tankers. But she remembered with a sinking heart that the birds had nearly always died, too weakened by their long ordeal to respond to treatment. For many, she knew, were oiled far out at sea, and drifted helplessly for days before being washed inshore.

The bird in front of her seemed lively enough, however, and when she stooped to touch him, he jabbed savagely at her outstretched hand with a sharply pointed beak. She stepped back hastily, deciding to run home and fetch the boys instead of attempting the rescue on her own.

But as she set off up the beach a little wave ran after her, and she realised that the tide had turned and was coming in steadily over the wide stretch of sand. She looked at the bird and saw him struggling to escape from the encroaching water. But his wings were heavily caked with oil and even his webbed feet were coated.

"Oh, you poor thing!" she cried pityingly, then caught her breath as she realised that she would have to catch this bird herself and carry it beyond the reach of the rising tide. Frantically she tried to remember the directions in the booklet, wishing she had paid more attention when Peter read them out.

Another wave washed round the bird and he stumbled awkwardly, trying to avoid it. Stella crept after him cautiously, but the moment she was within reach he jabbed at her as before. The next wave swept him off his feet and rolled him up the beach, leaving him floundering helplessly in a shallow pool. Forgetful of the long, sharp beak, Stella plunged after him and snatched him out of the water, since it was evident that he could no longer keep himself afloat. He turned on her immediately, more fiercely than before, but she bravely held on long enough to carry him beyond the reach of the next wave before dumping him on the beach. He was weaker than she had realised, and, despite the sharpness of his beak, his peck had been a feeble one, and her hand was merely scratched. Nevertheless she hated the thought of touching him again, and from the expression in his eyes she guessed that he hated it himself! But the tide was rising rapidly and, since the bird was unable to fly or swim, something would have to be done if his life were to be saved. She glanced hopefully round the beach, but everyone seemed to be picnicking down at the other end today, and there was nobody within earshot except a couple of boys playing with a dog. A dog was the last thing she wanted now, so obviously she would have to do the job entirely on her own.

Looking back, she saw that the sea was beginning to wash around her forgotten canvas bag. But she had more than laver-bread to worry about just now. Desperately she tried to remember the instructions in the booklet—surely there had been something about wrapping the birds in pieces of blanket? Perhaps she could use the canvas bag instead. It would be cold and comfortless of course, but it would at least protect her from that alarming beak. And once the bird was safely wrapped, she would be able to hurry it home to Peter, who would know what to do next.

She emptied the precious laverbread into the sea without another thought and started to edge towards the bird. But although he could neither swim nor fly he proved unexpectedly hard to catch, shuffling out of the way as she approached and lunging at her all the while with open beak. And yet, fierce as he was, he was clearly growing weaker. It was a distressing chase, and she was half-crying by the time she finally managed to envelop the exhausted bird in the canvas bag. As she gathered the bulky bundle into her arms she wondered that so large a bird should weigh so little. She did not realise that he was thin from near-starvation.

At first he struggled violently, then lay so still that she was afraid he must be dead. She stumbled on up the beach until his stillness became unbearable, and she simply had to stop and move the canvas aside an inch to see if he showed any sign of life. In an instant he was very much alive, fighting to free his vicious beak from the enveloping folds of the bag. Stella saw that it could only be a matter of minutes before he succeeded, since the bag was not quite big enough to cover him completely.

She also knew she would never be able to hold him once that beak was free. So she turned with a sob of sheer relief when she heard the sound of Sammy's voice behind her.

"Oh, Sammy, it's a guillemot, and he's covered with oil," she explained, realising with a surge of thankfulness that Sammy would know exactly what to do.

He knew so well that he took the bird calmly from her hands, freeing its head instead of covering it as she had tried to do. He seemed quite oblivious of pecks, despite the fact that his hands were soon bleeding in several places. After a few minutes his calmness seemed to communicate itself to the bird, and by the time they reached the cottage it had ceased to struggle.

Stella followed Sammy into the dark little kitchen of his home and watched him unwrap the bird in front of the fire.

"Ellygug" was all he said. She guessed this must be a country name for a guillemot, since he always chose such names for his birds, calling his one-legged jackdaw "Cawdaw" and every linnet "Lintie."

Having settled the bird in a blanket-lined box in front of the fire he got to his feet and shuffled towards the door, indicating with a jerk of his head that Stella should follow him.

"But aren't you going to clean him or feed him or anything?" she questioned, staring down at the bird.

Sammy made no answer, merely pausing to collect an empty jam jar from the cupboard as he went out.

Stella hung back, wondering if the bird should really be left like this, and, as she stood there uncertainly, the stair door opened and old Martha appeared round the turn of the stone spiral.

"Ah, the creature'll be all right with Sammy, whatever it is," she said confidently, answering Stella's unspoken doubts; then catching sight of the box by the fire, she added, "So it's an Ellygug this time, is it? You leave him be, he'll be all right, he's best getting over the worst of the shock in the warmth of the fire before he tries to eat. Sam's off to catch some fish for him now, no doubt."

"He did take a jar," said Stella.

"There you are, then! I'll say that for Sammy, he always knows just what to do where the creatures is concerned."

She followed Stella out into the sunshine and they stood for a moment in the shadow of the figurehead.

"Look, there he is now," said Martha, pointing to where the slouching figure ambled towards the rocks, the empty jam jar flashing in his hand. The old woman sighed as she watched him, murmuring under her breath, "I only wish I could be sure he'd take half such good care of himself as he does of his creatures." Then, turning to look at the wooden figure above them, she made a surprising remark.

"My brother always said that *Evelyn Starr* would take care of Sammy. I only hope he was right."

Stella saw to her amazement that the old woman was absolutely serious.

"*Evelyn Starr?*" she echoed. "But how could she possibly?"

"He never explained," said Martha simply, "but he believed it himself, that's certain. Many's the time he made me promise never to get rid of this old figurehead. 'She's all I have to leave the boy,' he used to say, 'and the Colonel's right, there could come a day when Sam might need the help that *Evelyn Starr* could give.' "

"But what help could she give?" persisted Stella doubtfully. "I mean, she's only made of wood."

Old Martha shook her head with a gentle smile.

"That's something I don't know, my dear," she answered. "All I know is that my brother believed it himself, and so did Colonel Griffiths up the Manor. Always fussing round her they were, touching her up with pots of paint and mending little bits that had got broken; thought the world of her, they did. I remember that last day how the Colonel says to me, 'Martha,' he says, serious-like, 'don't you ever let anyone take *Evelyn Starr* away, she's watched over your brother all these years, saving his life for him in the end, and now she holds poor Sam's security in the hollow of her hand.' I'll always remember the way he said those words, slow and kind of sad. To make him smile, I says—

" 'Well, sir,' I says, 'why ever would I be wanting to part with *Evelyn Starr*, now you've painted her up so nice, with all that gold on her jewellery and all.'

"But he didn't smile as I hoped he would, he only says, thoughtful-like, 'Odd you should say that, very odd indeed, since her jewellery could produce the help poor Sam might need one day. But—and remember this—I would never wish you to turn to *Evelyn Starr* for help unless Sam is in genuine trouble. You understand?'

"Dead serious he was, watching me straight with those eyes of his, and then he went on very quiet: 'Come outside now and I'll show you what I mean.'

"But when we came out we found Sammy here in the yard, and the Colonel changed his mind.

" 'Not just now,' he says to me quickly, under his breath, 'I'll tell you next time.'

"But there was never a next time, that was the last I ever saw of him. Next day he was gone, and my brother with him, drowned out there in the bay."

She stood for a moment longer, lost in a dream of the past, then turned and shuffled away indoors, having already forgotten Stella's existence.

As she made her way slowly home through the sand dunes, Stella felt as though she were returning from another world, far away in time and space, and it was a conscious effort to drag herself back to the world of everyday. Long Holm always had this effect on her; the place had a strange air of remoteness and tranquillity not to be found elsewhere. There was a mysterious atmosphere, too, about *Evelyn Starr,* marooned on shore after years of ocean voyaging, and even the small dark cottage crouched in her shadow had a distinct character of its own.

She would have much to tell them at home today about the rescue of the guillemot and the loss of the laverbread. But there were other things, those mysterious hints about *Evelyn Starr,* that she would not mention—perhaps to anyone.

Chapter 3

AT LAST it was time to go and meet Marie-Thérèse.

"I'm afraid you'll have to go in to the station by bus," said Mrs. Bevan. "Daddy won't be home in time with the car today."

"Never mind, the top of the bus is really best for seeing things," said Stella cheerfully. "I want to show her the castle and the bays as we come along."

"One of you boys had better go, too," suggested Mrs. Bevan. "After all, you are the ones who will recognise her."

"Oh, but Mum, that's a ghastly waste of time," objected Robert.

"I can't help that, she may have a heavy suitcase and need your help."

"As a matter of fact we could do with some more of that mahogany stopping," mused Peter, "and while you're in the shop you might as well get a couple more sheets of number-one sandpaper."

"I like that!" retorted Robert hotly. "Why take it for granted I'll be the one to go? Mum said one of us."

"Oh, be your age," growled Peter. "You know I want to give the spars their final coat of varnish and this is a perfect drying day, much too good to waste in town."

Robert opened his mouth to argue, but thought better of it and merely said, "Well I just hope Marie-Thérèse speaks English as well as Philippe did—d'you know, Mum, he was almost word-perfect by the time we left, honestly he was."

"That I can well believe," said his mother dryly. "I only wish you and Peter had learnt half as much French in the time. As far as I can gather you spoke nothing but English all the while you were there!"

"Ah, but Philippe was dead keen to learn English you see, and he was so quick it really was fun to teach him."

"I don't doubt it, but we didn't pay all that money for you to go to France as teachers," his mother reminded him severely. "Now Marie-Thérèse is coming here to learn English naturally, but I certainly hope that when Stella goes to France next year she will remember that she is there to learn French and not teach anybody English! But now you'd better get moving or you'll miss that bus."

The bus was a double-decker, and Robert and Stella got their favourite front seats on top. All the way into town Stella sat in a trance, trying to see the familiar coastline through the eyes of Marie-Thérèse, and planning what to show her on the return journey.

From the bus depot they went straight to a fascinating shop known as Captain Morgan's Store. A steering wheel hung over the door, and the showroom contained everything from canoes and sailing dinghies down to the least of their owners' requirements. There were anchors and flags and riding lights, as well as a wide range of duller articles such as shackles, rope and screws. There was also a case of books on sailing and fishing, and Stella was studying these when Robert called her across to look at something else.

"Isn't it a beauty?" he exclaimed, pointing to a secondhand telescope. "It's got a wonderful lens, I've just had a look, and it's in pretty good condition too. Three pounds is wonderful value for a powerful lens like that."

"Are you going to start saving up for it?" asked Stella.

"Hardly likely it'd still be here by the time I managed to save all that," he replied, and picking up his parcels he turned towards the door.

They got to the station five minutes before the train was due. They found a vacant seat on the platform and Robert was soon absorbed in various pamphlets he had picked up in the shop.

Stella sat beside him, and as she waited she became uncomfortably conscious of a fluttery feeling starting in the pit of her stomach. For the first time she faced the fact that Marie-Thérèse was nearly four years older than herself and might well turn out to be very grown-up, with lots of make-up and a grand Parisian hair style—the sort of person who might easily look on Stella as no more than a boring little girl. By the time the train drew in she was feeling almost sick with dread.

Suddenly Robert sprang away from her side and shouted to someone in the thick of the crowd who were pouring along the platform.

"Why, she looks just like a boy!" was Stella's first thought, and a wave of relief swept over her. There was no grand hair style, no make-up, just a close-cropped head and a skinny figure in shirt and jeans with a rucksack instead of a suitcase.

But her relief was short-lived; as the two drew near to where she was standing she saw that the newcomer really was a boy a year or so older than herself.

"Philippe's come after all," explained Robert introducing them. "Marie-Thérèse sprained her ankle very badly a couple of days ago, so Madame Griveau wrote to Mummy asking if we'd mind if Philippe came after all—she said send a wire if we did mind."

"But Mummy's never had a letter!" objected Stella, struggling to hide her bitter disappointment.

"I know, I expect it got held up by the postal strike or something. Anyway, he'll be another to help with the boat which will be wonderful, he's done heaps of sailing, haven't you Philippe. Come on, let's go."

Stella trailed along behind the boys in utter dejection. She quite forgot her recent nervousness and was only conscious of the fact that here was yet another boy to hang around the boatshed, leaving her to amuse herself on her own, as before.

The journey home was very different from the one that she had planned. They sat on top of the bus, and the front seats were empty as she had hoped they would be. But this no longer mattered, since she found herself sitting alone with the rucksack, while the two boys sat in the opposite seat, so deep in conversation that it wasn't worth trying to point out anything; she very much doubted they would even have heard if she had spoken!

When they got home, Mrs. Bevan met them at the door with a thin foreign envelope in her hand.

"This has just arrived by the afternoon post from your mother," she said, hurrying forward to welcome Philippe with a smile.

"I hope it does not make a difficulty for you?" he asked a trifle anxiously as he shook hands.

"No, indeed, we are delighted to have you; after all, you are the one we originally expected. Poor Marie-Thérèse, though, I hope her ankle isn't very painful?"

Philippe shrugged expressively.

"It was her own fault," he explained. "She had high heels and she tried to run, so . . . !" He left the sentence unfinished, spreading his hands in a gesture of resignation.

"The only thing is, I'm afraid you will find your room rather flowery and feminine since it was prepared for your sister, but I don't suppose you'll mind that," said Mrs. Bevan.

With a rush of fury Stella remembered her favourite books arranged on the shelf by the visitor's bed and the special pictures lent from her own room. There was no time to move them now, and she didn't suppose this boy would even notice them. He certainly wouldn't appreciate them, of that she was sure.

The boys swept Philippe straight out to the shed to see the boat. Stella hung back, but her mother slipped an arm round her shoulders with a quick little hug of sympathy.

"You go too, dear," she insisted, pushing her towards the door.

For the next few days the boys spent all their time in the shed where Peter and Robert explained details of the job to their new recruit. He knew far more about boats than they did, and on a considerably larger scale, since many of his relations were seamen, and during the holidays he spent most of his time on his uncle's boat in Roscoff harbour.

This was, however, the first time he had had anything to do with building a boat, and although he knew the position and purpose of every part, he had never before attempted to fit these together. To everyone's surprise, including his own, he proved a slow and clumsy pupil. By the fourth day Stella became aware of an undercurrent of irritation, as her brothers exchanged exasperated glances over their visitor's head. She noticed that Philippe was given the dull jobs, just as she herself had been when she tried to help. Her mother noticed, too, and watched the trio anxiously.

"I do hope that boy is happy," she murmured.

Stella remembered her own days in the shed.

"I suppose there may be some boys, as well as girls, who don't specially like building boats, even if they do like sailing," she suggested.

Mrs. Bevan considered this before replying. "Look here, I have an idea. We never gave him that laverbread, remember? So how about suggesting that he go to the rocks with you to get some now? The tide is low, I see. And you could show him *Evelyn Starr* as well, he might be interested."

"Oh, yes, and Long Holm, too," added Stella enthusiastically.

Next time Philippe passed the window they called him in. When he heard of the proposed expedition his eyes crinkled up at the corners in the way they did when he was specially interested in something.

"I must fill this bucket for Peter first, and then I come with you; I've been wanting to see those rocks down there," he answered.

When they reached the rocks Philippe soon lost interest in the laverbread and began poking in pools and crevices, collecting various shellfish which he assured her would be good to eat.

Stella looked them over dubiously.

"Ugh! No—they look disgusting!" she exclaimed, frowning at the assortment in his hands.

"But yes, they are good, these," he insisted. "I will show you. I will cook them myself if Mrs. Bevan does not like them, and you will see."

Stella soon had all the laverbread she could be bothered to pick.

"Now come and see the Holm," she suggested, leading the way out onto the low rocky causeway that linked the main mass of Long Holm to the mainland at low water. "When the tide is high all this becomes an island," she explained. "And the very highest tides of all turn it into three separate little islands—you can see it has three humps like a sea serpent with grass and flowers growing on top of each. The water never comes up over that greenery although it covers the rocks between."

Then, glancing sideways at her companion she went on a trifle hesitantly, "The boys and I have always pretended the islands belong to the three of us, one each," she explained. Then, seeing that Philippe was not at all scornful of such a fanciful idea, she continued—

"The big one is Peter's. It's the only place round here where you can find yellow horned poppies. But he really bagged it because of the birds: ringed plovers nest out there and sometimes oystercatchers, too.

"The middle one is Robert's. That's got something special, too; it's the only place we know for cowrie shells.

"Then the rocky one out there at the end is mine!" she finished on a note of pride.

"And has yours got something special, too?" he asked, looking out towards the farthest rocks.

"I should just say it has—it's the most exciting of them all!" she smiled. "I won't tell you what it is, I'll show you. Come on! Mind you!" she went on, as they picked their way out over the slippery causeway, "we didn't know the secret of my island when we chose which ones we'd have, or I'd never have been allowed to have it. Robert would have bagged it for certain, he's always trying to make me swap as it is."

"When do you come to these islands?" asked Philippe, slithering over the weed-grown rocks behind her.

"Oh, it's only really worth it when the weather's pretty settled, there's no shelter at all on the boys' islands you see. And once you're cut off out here you can't get back for about four hours. Oh! But it's gorgeous when it's fine enough to do it; it's such fun being out here all on our own, knowing that nobody can call us away or come to us for four whole hours!"

"And can you get from one island to the other when the tide is high?" he asked.

"Yes, most of the time. There's just about an hour at the top of the highest floods of all, when the water gets a bit too deep between them. That's an exciting feeling, being the only person on a desert island! I like looking out to sea then, and pretending I'm really a castaway, wondering if I'll ever be rescued! If it's hazy weather—which it often is when it's really fine of course—then sometimes you can't even see across to Devon. That makes it really seem like a desert island, miles away from anywhere, with only that old bell buoy for company in a boundless waste of sea—oh, it's a wonderful feeling!"

She drew his attention to the chief attractions of each island in turn. The first two were edged with miniature beaches of coarse sand littered with broken limpet shells and fragments of blue mussel shell. Above the sand the rocks were topped with springy lawns of rough grass among which grew dandelions and white sea campion and a few bedraggled daisies. In addition, Peter's island boasted a large patch of yellow horned poppies, although most of the golden petals were gone now, and there was little to see save the long green horns that gave the plant its name.

"I'm afraid we're too late for the birds' nests, too," said Stella apologetically.

But she found that Philippe was not specially interested anyway, assuring her that they had the same birds and flowers around the coasts of Brittany. Nor did he bother with Robert's cowries, despite the fact that she picked up three straightaway without even having to look for them.

The third island lay some distance from the other two and was totally different in character, being little more than a mass of angular rocks upthrust from the end of the peninsula. There was no lawn here, and very little greenery, the sparse plant life being mainly composed of clumps of thrift and the scented samphire that clung to whatever crevices could be found among the rocks.

Stella led the way across a deep gully which echoed with resounding "plops" as their moving shadows startled the fish temporarily stranded in the shallow tidal pools. The final bastion of rock fell away in a long sweep to an even deeper gully beyond which flat rocks, dark with seaweed and deep pools, ran out to meet the sea. Just offshore the bell buoy rocked on the slow swell, its deep clang sounding now and again on the fitful breeze. Philippe glanced back to the boys' green islands, wondering what this wild place could have to offer in comparison.

"Here it is!" called Stella, and looking down he saw that she was making her way along an irregular ledge that crossed the rocky face of the height on which he was standing. A moment later, with a triumphant upward glance at him, she stooped and vanished into the cliff face.

Philippe was after her in a flash, scrambling along the ledge until he came to the entrance to a cave. He crawled in after her and found himself in a small, low-ceilinged chamber hollowed out of the solid rock. The earth floor was dry and dusty, proving that even the highest tides never came as high as this. In the confined space the clang of the buoy was amplified, ringing out like the bell of some country church. He could not see it from where he sat, however, the ledge of rock outside the entrance cutting off all sight of everything except a wide sweep of the horizon, and a clear view of the Devon coast lying scarcely more than twenty miles away across the channel.

"*Merveilleux!*" he exclaimed, forgetting his proudly acquired English in the excitement of the moment.

"And the best of it is, you can't see this cave from absolutely anywhere," said Stella. "You might, I suppose, from a ship at sea, but it can't be seen from anywhere on land. That's what makes it so secret, of course, and that's why we never guessed it was here until I explored my island properly."

"You could live in here you know," Philippe declared. "I wonder if anyone ever has?"

"I've never heard of it," she admitted reluctantly. "But then it's such a secret place, we mightn't ever know if it had been used, might we?"

Philippe was too preoccupied to reply at once.

"There'd be shellfish to eat," he mused presently, "plenty of crabs and lobsters down there in those pools, I bet! Only there would be no water, of course."

"Well, that would be easy, actually," said Stella. "You could go ashore at low tide and get it from the well at the back of Sammy's cottage—come on, I'll show you where it is. We'd better be moving anyway, the tide turned some time ago, and I certainly don't want to be stuck out here for four hours with nothing to eat but those awful shellfish! Besides, I want to show you *Evelyn Starr*."

The tide had risen considerably and the causeway was very much narrower than when they had crossed over, proving that it was just as well they turned back when they did.

As they walked along the shore towards Sammy's cottage they followed an intriguing tide line in which innumerable odds and ends were mingled with the usual mass of seaweed and tarred cork.

"Oh, look!" cried Stella, pouncing on a yellow plastic Indian complete with tomahawk. "This must have come out of a cereal box. I'll take it along to Sammy, he'll be thrilled."

"Sammy?" questioned Philippe, looking up from the tide line with a puzzled frown, "but I thought . . . what age has this Sammy then?"

"I'm not quite sure, older than Mummy, anyway."

"So . . . I do not understand . . ." Philippe glanced again at the toy in her hand, looking more confused than ever.

"Of course! I forgot you haven't even seen Sammy yet," said Stella. "Well, you see, he's just a little bit simple."

"Simple?" Philippe lingered a moment over the unfamiliar use of a word he knew with a different meaning. But before he had time to work it out he caught sight of the figurehead leaning out from the cottage wall, and it swept all other thoughts from his mind.

"So! From a ship," he remarked, smiling up at the carved wooden face. "And what is it you call her?"

"*Evelyn Starr*."

"Ah, yes, I know, I hear you speak of *Evelyn Starr* before. But what word have you for what she is?"

"Oh, I see what you mean, she's a figurehead."

"Ah, so, a figurehead," he repeated, nodding slowly as he memorised the new word.

A tuneless humming attracted their attention and standing on tiptoe Stella looked over the wall into the small paved enclosure that fronted the cottage in place of a garden. This tiny yard was littered with all sorts of wreckage from the beach; there were corks and wood for burning, boxes and baskets that would come in handy one day, and a fine rope fender waiting to be emptied of its cork filling, and flattened into a doormat such as lay in every porch in the village. There were also glass balls and metal floats and a hundred useless objects that Sammy had been unable to resist when he found them washed ashore. He was sorting some of these treasures now, his wordless humming proof of his deep contentment.

"Hallo, Sammy!" called Stella over the wall. "How's Elly-gug? Oh, I say, he looks better, doesn't he?" she added as the guillemot waddled into view at the sound of a strange voice.

"Ah," said Sammy, "oil's not all off him yet, though, takes

time, that does." Then, noticing Philippe for the first time, he was too overcome with shyness to say another word. But he did delve into his pocket and pull out a long strip of fish which the bird, edging closer in hopes of a second helping, snatched from his fingers. Sammy beamed with pride, watching his visitors out of the side of his eye to make sure they were properly impressed.

Stella saw that there was no hope of inducing Sammy to tell them any more, so she gave him the plastic toy instead, and enquired after Willie. Sammy's hand went into his pocket again, but instead of the expected mouse he brought out a squirming slow worm and held it out to her. Philippe eyed her with some admiration as she took the snakelike creature in her hand.

"You'd never get my sister Marie-Thérèse to touch a thing like that," he remarked.

"Oh, but this isn't a snake you know; slow worms don't hurt anyone," she said, spreading her fingers to allow the twisting creature to flow between them. "Poor thing, it's doing its best to terrify us now, trying to look like a snake," and she pointed to the blue forked tongue that was flickering in and out of its open mouth in a brave attempt at intimidation.

"Ellygug looks horribly interested, you won't let him get at it, will you?" she said as she handed the reptile back to Sammy who merely pocketed it without another word.

As they walked home across the beach, Philippe said thoughtfully, "So that is what you call 'simple'—*un enfant de bon Dieu.*"

"A *what*?" demanded Stella stopping abruptly, not quite believing what she thought she had heard him say.

"I said that Sammy is *un enfant de bon Dieu*—a child of the Good Lord," he answered casually.

"Why ever do you call him that?" she asked curiously.

"Because that is our name for those ones in Brittany," replied Philippe, surprised in his turn. "When they are a little bit 'simple' as you say. Do you not also call them 'children of God'?"

Stella shook her head slowly.

"I don't think so, I've never heard it, anyway. But it's an awfully nice name, isn't it, specially for someone who's as nice as dear old Sammy. And he's simply marvellous with animals, you know."

"Ah, but that is why he has that gift, of course," said Philippe. "Those simple ones have special powers that the rest of us do not have. With Sammy it is a gift with animals. And who takes care of Sammy himself?"

"His old Aunt Martha. His mother died when he was a baby, so Aunt Martha brought him up. She's awfully old now, though, and we really think Sammy does most of the looking after nowadays. He's not half as stupid as people sometimes think."

"They've a grand little home there anyway; I should like to live right on the shore like that myself," remarked Philippe, turning for a final glimpse of the cottage before following Stella into the sand dunes that lay between the village and the bay.

"Ah, yes, that's one of the Manor cottages," she said. "They're lucky to have it. Hundreds of people would give anything to buy it for a holiday place, it's in such a gorgeous situation. But Mr. Griffiths allows the Walters to go on living there because his father, old Colonel Griffiths, let Sammy's father have it. I think they were great friends when they were boys or something. And then," she mused, trying to recall a half-remembered tale, "I believe both their wives died at the same time or something—Mummy has told me, but I forget exactly what did happen."

Chapter 4

PHILIPPE was not one to forget anything which contained the promise of a story, and directly they got home he went in search of Mrs. Bevan. He found her in the dining room, packing an enormous hamper full of things for a forthcoming jumble sale.

"Mrs. Bevan, please," he began, "can you tell me the story of Sammy and his father? Stella began to tell me but she couldn't remember it all."

"Why, how nice to find you interested," said Mrs. Bevan, smiling with pleasure. "You see I was born and brought up in this village myself, my father was the doctor here, so it's always nice when someone wants to know about the place.

"Well, I expect Stella told you that Captain Walters, Sammy's father, was skipper of a little trading schooner called *Evelyn Starr?*"

"Yes, she told me that," replied Philippe, watching Stella as she crouched beside the open hamper, turning over the contents. Mrs. Bevan's gaze strayed away beyond the open window as she went on—

"And no doubt she also told you of his lifelong friendship with Colonel Griffiths who owned the Manor House and most of the surrounding land and cottages."

"Mummy!" Stella's shocked exclamation broke into the story and they looked round to see her sitting back on her heels beside the hamper with a limp cloth panda in her hand.

"Mummy," she repeated accusingly, "you surely weren't going to send Pandy to the jumble sale? You couldn't have been."

"Now, don't be silly, darling," said her mother shortly. "You haven't given him a thought for years, and you would never have remembered him again if you hadn't come across him now."

"But, Mum, I found him on the high tide, don't you remember, and Daddy helped me to clean off all the tar. I couldn't let him go."

"Well, keep him up in your room then, he's not going back into the cupboard under the stairs, do you understand? And for goodness' sake leave the rest of those things alone. Now, Philippe, where was I?"

"You were saying that Sammy's father and the Colonel were good friends," he prompted.

"Ah yes. You see they had grown up here in the village together as boys, and being about the same age did everything together. Even when they grew up and married and went their different ways their friendship continued unbroken, and they always made a point of meeting whenever the Captain was at home between voyages."

"Good to have a friend like that for all your life," mused Philippe.

"Yes indeed. And as things turned out they were to need that friendship very badly. For just when everything seemed at its most promising, each man with a happy home and a newborn baby son, a violent epidemic of flu swept through the village, carrying off almost as many young people as old. Amongst others it took the two young wives of Colonel Griffiths and Captain Walters."

"Oh, no!" cried Philippe with such intensity that Stella found herself caught up in the story, too, and leaning back against the hamper she fixed her eyes on her mother's face as though she, too, were hearing it all for the first time.

"Yes, it was a terrible tragedy," agreed Mrs. Bevan. "It was before my time of course, but it was talked about for many a long year, since both men were well liked in the district.

"Strangely enough the two babies survived, although Colonel Griffiths' little Hubert caught the complaint and very nearly died as well."

"You'd never guess it to look at him now, would you?" said Stella. "That is our Mr. Griffiths, isn't it?"

Mrs. Bevan nodded and took up the story again.

"Poor Captain Walters was half the world away at the time, and when he returned it was to find his cottage empty and neglected and his baby far away in Wiltshire, being cared for by its grandmother.

"When he made enquiries about his friend he learnt that Colonel Griffiths had shut up the Manor and gone into lodgings in Carmarthen with a couple of old servants, refusing even to see his little son who was kept in the kitchen quarters."

"You'd think the baby would have been a comfort, wouldn't you?" mused Stella.

"Captain Walters evidently thought so too, and took matters into his own hands at once. Ignoring the scared old servants he marched straight past them into the Colonel's private sitting room. What took place at that meeting was never known, of course, but as a direct result of it the Manor was reopened and became a normal home once more, although the Colonel never married again. New servants were engaged and a new young nurse was soon seen about the village with baby Hubert, a fine, bonny little fellow, obviously quite recovered from his recent illness.

"And so, by the time the Captain returned to sea, he was able to feel that for his friend, at any rate, things were looking better. It would be time enough to put his own home in order when he returned from his next voyage."

The story was interrupted here by the entrance of Peter and Robert, coming to see if there was any sign of tea.

"Not for another half hour at least," said Mrs. Bevan firmly. "I've all this jumble to attend to first."

Robert helped himself to an apple from the sideboard, then strolled across to look into the hamper.

"Pity to let that jersey go," he commented. "It'd be just the thing for the boat."

"Oh, Robert, surely you've all the jerseys you need," protested his mother. "Besides, I do so loathe that hideous garment; it doesn't fit you anywhere and I've always hated the colour."

Peter pounced on a coverless book.

"That's where it's got to!" he cried triumphantly. "I've hunted everywhere for this old bird book."

"But you've got a whole shelf of bird books," objected his mother.

"Ah, but this one's out on its own when it comes to local names—listen to this: 'Cherubim' for a barn owl, 'Cockandy' for a puffin," and flipping through the pages he read out several more at random.

Mrs. Bevan got to her feet in a sudden swift movement of exasperation, and, sweeping the carefully sorted piles of books and clothing off chairs and table, she dumped them higgledy-piggledy into the hamper and shut down the lid decisively.

"That'll have to do," she said with a sigh, "I can't be bothered with any more sorting now. Take the basket out to the garage, will you boys, I'll drive it round to the vicarage when the car comes back. In the meantime I'll see about some tea."

Philippe and Stella followed her into the kitchen, and as soon as she settled down to cut the sandwiches they propped themselves against the table, one on either side of her.

"Now, please," urged Philippe. "Will you tell us the rest of the story?"

"Story? What story?" murmured Mrs. Bevan absently, her mind occupied with the pepper and salt she was sprinkling over the first layer of cucumber.

"Oh, Mum, you know, about Sammy's father," prompted Stella, adding persuasively, "couldn't you tell us while you're cutting these? You were just coming to the bit about what happened when old Captain Walters came home from his next voyage."

"He wasn't all that old at the time," said her mother, smiling. "But like his friend, he never married again. His sister Martha left the people with whom she was in service in the North, and came down here to look after him, and baby Sammy was fetched home from Wiltshire to live with them. But already it was obvious that the poor little fellow would never be quite like other children."

"D'you know," interrupted Stella, "Philippe says that in Brittany they call people like Sammy 'children of God,' isn't that a nice name for them?"

"It certainly is, and especially appropriate for Sammy who was such a lovable little chap. His Aunt Martha was absolutely devoted to him from the start."

"So, in a way, it all worked out pretty well, didn't it?" murmured Stella who hated stories with unhappy endings.

"I suppose so, in a way," admitted her mother a trifle doubtfully, "although the poor Captain's troubles were by no means over, you remember. While Sammy was still little more than a child the *Evelyn Starr* was wrecked, and as you know nothing was saved except the figurehead."

"But that was lucky in a sort of way," insisted Stella, "because after all it was *Evelyn Starr* herself who really saved his life, wasn't it? I'll tell you that bit later," she promised Philippe quickly, "only we must hear the rest of Mummy's story now."

"Well, there isn't much more to tell," said Mrs. Bevan, pushing aside the plate of sandwiches. "Now, Philippe, would you like the next lot to be paste or tomato?"

"Paste, please," he answered, passing her the jar. "And did the Captain get another boat?"

"No, he never went back to sea again. He turned his hand to carpentry instead and stayed at home, making quite a tolerable living. He also sold crabs and lobsters as a side line, I remember.

"Anyway, one very satisfactory result of his retirement from the sea was the deepening of his friendship with Colonel Griffiths who spent more and more time at the shore cottage. It was he who helped to erect the figurehead where it stands today. The two of them spent hours fussing over her like a couple of dear old nannies, replacing and repairing bits that had been damaged in the shipwreck. As to the painting, you never saw anything like it; the older villagers remember a time when all those heavy jewels glittered like real gems. Martha often used to laugh about it with my mother, not that she minded what they did so long as they were happily occupied. She was very fond of Colonel Griffiths and so was Sammy, with whom he was always extraordinarily gentle. He often sighed as he watched the child, and Martha fancied he was regretting the fact that his own son and his friend's son, although the same age, could never be the companions their fathers had been.

"It was at the end of one of these visits that he appears to have told Martha never to part with the figurehead."

"Yes, she told me that," interrupted Stella. "He told her that *Evelyn Starr* would always look after Sammy, because she holds his security in the hollow of her hand—I think that was the way he said it."

"Yes, that's right," said Mrs. Bevan. "And even after all these years she still attaches tremendous importance to what, I am sure, was largely a sentimental attachment to a relic of happier days. Also he may have realized that the figurehead would increase in value through the years. No doubt his words made a particularly deep impression because it was the last time he spoke to her before his tragic death."

"Ah, now that was the bit I couldn't remember properly," said Stella. "What happened to him exactly?"

"He was drowned, poor man, and the Captain with him. They decided to borrow a friend's boat and go out after the mackerel that had been in and out of the bay all the week. But just as they cleared the headland a squall sprang up and upset the boat and the men were unable to reach the shore, encumbered as they were with heavy clothes and rubber boots."

"Well, at least I'm glad they went together and never had to be parted," murmured Stella.

"It's a pity, though, that poor old Martha took the Colonel's words so literally," mused her mother. "I believe it's unusual to find a figurehead wearing such elaborate jewellery, and because of this *Evelyn Starr* is something of a collectors' piece. I know Martha has had some really tantalising offers for her."

Stella swung round in shocked amazement.

"You mean she ought to sell *Evelyn Starr*? Mummy, how could you even think of anything so awful?"

Her mother's reply was quietly reasonable.

"I know, I'd hate to see her go myself," she admitted. "All the same poor old Martha needs all the money she can lay her hands on. Her little pension and the bit she gets for Sammy doesn't go very far these days, you know."

Philippe looked up. "But if she is really needing help for Sammy, then might this be the time to take what the figurehead holds?" he suggested slowly.

"Oh, you don't quite understand, that's merely an English figure of speech, a sort of saying," Mrs. Bevan explained. "She doesn't actually hold anything; I think the Colonel merely guessed that she was likely to become a valuable object in time, and wanted to impress on Martha the importance of keeping her until she could be sure of commanding a really satisfactory price if it should ever be necessary to sell her."

Philippe said nothing, but from the look on his face Stella felt pretty certain that he agreed with Martha. Presently he asked another question: "And what about Colonel Griffiths' son, is he a good man like his father?"

"We don't see a great deal of him, since our house is one of the few that does not belong to the Manor estate. Some people complain that he is inclined to be hard, but at the same time they all agree that whatever he does is purely done for the good of the estate, which he runs exactly as it was run in his father's day. There are bound to be grumbles now and then, of course; nevertheless I know everyone would really agree that Mr. Griffiths is the right man in the right place."

Stella glanced across at Philippe who was leaning against the table, his dark eyes intent on her mother's face. She had never seen anyone pay such close attention to a story. Philippe evidently threw himself into the business of listening as wholeheartedly as he threw himself into anything else that caught his interest. The mere sight of his rapt face fired her own imagination, giving the old story a strange new interest.

Before the week was over this interest was sharply revived.

Chapter 5

THE mingled smells of laverbread and varnish filled the house and garden. The pungent smell of the laverbread came from a large preserving pan that bubbled quietly, hour after hour, on the back of the kitchen stove. Philippe was as keen as the rest of them about this strange sea food, and he and Stella had made another trip to the rocks to gather it. On the way home they had called again at Sammy's cottage to see how Ellygug was getting on. Philippe had also taken several snapshots of *Evelyn Starr*, saving the rest of the roll for the boat.

And she really was a boat at last, complete except for her final coat of varnish. Everyone was excited now and Philippe and Stella had been called in to help in the final stages, since they were all determined to get her launched before Philippe's visit came to an end.

They were all in the shed rubbing her down with sandpaper in preparation for this last important coat. Stella glanced up from her work for a moment to enjoy the busy scene, but was instantly reprimanded by Peter—

"For goodness' sake, look what you're doing, Stella," he cautioned. "You must keep rubbing with the grain of the wood or you'll ruin the whole effect."

At any other time she would have flashed out in anger, but now Philippe caught her eye and winked, and the moment passed with nothing to disturb the steady rhythm of the rubbing.

Eventually, even Peter was satisfied.

"Now!" he announced. "We must keep the place absolutely free of dust for this last stage. Better take off that woollen pullover, Philippe, and chuck it outside; we don't want anything fluffy in here for the present. We must sprinkle the floor with water, too, to lay the dust; the least speck could spoil this final coat."

Robert picked up a bucket at once and proceeded to scatter handfuls of water about the floor, while Peter dampened a cloth with turpentine substitute and removed every last vestige of wood dust from the surface of the boat itself. Stella made sure that the door and window were properly fastened, knowing what damage windblown dust and flying seeds might do.

At first they were almost afraid to breathe as they started brushing on the all-important final coat of varnish, but as they got into the swing of the work they relaxed and were soon talking again as usual.

"We'll absolutely have to decide what to call her soon," ventured Stella, introducing a topic over which there had already been many arguments.

"How about *Evelyn Starr?*" suggested Philippe, whose mind was still turning over the story he had heard. But the Bevans had known the figurehead all their lives and wanted something less familiar for their boat.

"Besides," objected Stella, "the *Evelyn Starr* was wrecked—we wouldn't want to name our boat after a wreck. Anyway it must be something beautiful and romantic like *Flying Spray* or *Ocean Breeze*."

"A bird's name would be nicer still," said Peter; "*Stormy Petrel*, say, or *Albatross*."

"I'd rather something exciting like *Wanderer* or *Explorer* or *Venturer*," declared Robert.

"What about *Wandering Gull* then, that's a bit of each," suggested Stella. "What do you think, Philippe?"

"*Evelyn Starr*," repeated Philippe obstinately.

This might well have developed into one of the usual family arguments if Mrs. Bevan had not come hurrying across the yard and burst in upon them just as things were becoming heated.

"Mum, whatever is it?" demanded Peter, all thought of dust from the open door swept away by the sight of her face.

"Old Martha Walters has died," she answered.

"Oh, poor old Sammy!" they exclaimed in chorus, "whatever will he do?"

"I simply can't imagine," replied their mother. "In any case I think I'd better slip down there now and see how he is, and if there is anything I can do. Try and notice if the phone rings, will you, and when the baker comes take two brown and a white."

The varnishing went ahead in a subdued silence, broken by speculations as to what was likely to become of Sammy.

"They'll never allow him to stay on by himself in the cottage, that's certain," said Peter gloomily. "I bet they'll send him up to the old people's hostel."

"Oh, but Peter, they can't—think of Ellygug and all his other creatures!" cried Stella.

"I know, but at least they're wild, so I suppose they could fend for themselves if they had to."

"Ellygug couldn't possibly, he follows Sammy absolutely everywhere now. Besides, he's not been back into the water yet," said Stella. "And think of poor old one-legged Cawdaw after all these years with Sammy. Oh! And Willie, poor little Willie! Would they ever let him keep a mouse in his pocket up there at the hostel, I wonder?"

"I bet some beastly summer visitor will get the shore cottage," growled Robert resentfully.

"Oh, but *Evelyn Starr*, what about her? The visitors must never have her!" cried Stella fiercely.

Philippe spoke for the first time.

"The visitors must not turn Sammy out of his cottage," he said unexpectedly. "Colonel Griffiths meant him to stay there for all his life, I'm sure he did. I think this must be what he meant when he talked about real trouble. I think the time has come when *Evelyn Starr* must give her help."

Peter looked up with a half-smile.

"Oh, but that's only a sort of a legend, you know," he explained. "Obviously a figurehead couldn't really do anything, could it?"

"But she must do something, that's what she is being kept for," said Philippe simply.

"Don't be mad. How could an old wooden figure possibly do a thing!" burst out Robert impatiently.

"Captain Walters believed she could, and so did Martha," Philippe pointed out. His tone was so quietly confident that Stella realised that he himself believed it too. And suddenly, to her own surprise, she discovered that she was also half convinced.

"He may be right," she faltered.

Robert rounded on her with renewed irritation.

"Oh, for goodness' sake," he snapped, "it's only an old story as you very well know. Philippe hasn't cottoned on to a figure of speech, that's all."

Philippe said nothing, but watching his face Stella was certain that he had understood every word. She also knew that he firmly believed that in some as yet unexplained way *Evelyn Starr* really would look after Sammy.

"Well, I believe it, too—now," she insisted defiantly.

"Oh, be your age," muttered Peter. "Pass me that bottle of thinner, will you, and add a few drops to this. Steady. O.K., that's enough. And try to remember that this is Wales in the twentieth century, not some soppy magic land where figureheads come to life."

No more was said and the work went on in silence, only interrupted by brief commands from Peter in connection with the job in hand.

By teatime the final coat of varnish was complete and nothing further could be done until it was dry. After pausing a moment to admire the beauty of the finished boat, they tiptoed out of the shed, careful to avoid kicking up any dust as they went out and shutting the door securely behind them.

They wandered round to the front of the house and there found Mrs. Bevan laying tea on a table on the lawn.

"How's Sammy?" asked Stella at once.

"He's taking it surprisingly well," replied her mother. "I don't think it's made much impression on him at all, not so far anyway. He's really more concerned about his slow worm which disappeared a couple of days ago."

The slam of a car door on the far side of the house heralded the return of Mr. Bevan, and a moment later he joined them in the garden.

"Bad business about old Martha," he remarked as he sat down.

"What d'you suppose will happen to Sammy, Dad?" asked Stella.

"Oh, he'll go to the hostel, obviously," replied her father calmly.

"But why can't he stay in the cottage? He did the cooking and the fires and everything when Martha was ill, or even tired, she told me so herself. She said there wasn't a thing he couldn't do—'real handy in the house' was what she called him."

"I'm quite ready to believe it, Sam's a good deal smarter than he looks. All the same, they'll never leave him there on his own, I'm sure of that. Besides, I believe Mr. Griffiths has had some really impressive offers for that cottage on account of its unique situation. He'd never have dreamt of selling it while old Martha was alive, of course, but Sammy's a different proposition altogether. Don't you fret about him, old dear, I'm sure he'll be perfectly happy in the hostel; they're wonderfully good to them there, you know, and Sammy's sure to enjoy the company. Added to which he'll be better fed than he's been for years. You mark my words, he'll settle down in no time."

"Not without his creatures, he won't, and they won't settle either," mumbled Stella. To her fury she heard an ominous quiver creep into her voice and dared not risk another word for fear of disgracing herself in front of the boys. Instead, she helped herself to a bun she didn't want and bit into it savagely.

The conversation went on around the table. Only Philippe sat in a silence as preoccupied as her own. Presently, under cover of the general conversation he leant across to remark, "I still think *Evelyn Starr* will manage something. I mean to go and examine her tomorrow—will you come, too?"

But Mrs. Bevan overheard the suggestion, and before Stella had time to reply she intervened.

"I think you'd all better keep away until after the funeral," she said quietly. "There are far too many people in and out of the cottage as it is. They're all being wonderfully kind, with offers of help, and they've brought more puddings and cakes than poor Sammy could eat in a week. But I think in the circumstances it would be kinder not to add to the congestion for the present."

"O.K.," said Philippe, bringing out what he felt to be one of his most successful English expressions. But after tea he confided to Stella that after the funeral would be too late.

"You see, I'm going home on Friday," he reminded her.

"Not this *next* Friday? Oh, Philippe, I didn't realise it was so soon, I thought we'd have another whole week after this one. Let's ask Mummy if you can't stay a bit longer."

But Philippe shook his head.

"Nope," he said, using another word he fancied. "My father would not permit it."

"Why ever not?"

"He would say that if there was a chance of an extra visit it should be for Marie-Thérèse to come. I've had her holiday already, you see. Her ankle is well now, so she would have to come. My papa thinks all the world of Marie-Thérèse, she's the only girl, you understand."

Stella was surprised at the change in herself. At the beginning of the holidays she could think of no one but Marie-Thérèse. But now she was merely a stranger, and one that Stella did not even particularly wish to meet. For Marie-Thérèse could never be half as good a companion as her brother, that was very certain.

"I wish we could think of some plan so that you could stay!" she cried, clenching her fists fiercely.

"I wish too," echoed Philippe, but he did not sound very hopeful.

Chapter 6

THE launching was planned for Thursday to give the varnish plenty of time to dry. But during Wednesday night the weather changed, and when they woke on Thursday morning it was to the lash of rain driven against the windows by a gale-force wind.

"I don't see much hope of launching the boat in this, even by this evening," grumbled Peter, slumping into his chair at the breakfast table.

Mr. Bevan laid aside his paper.

"Now, look here, Pete, and the rest of you, too. There can be no question of launching the boat today, understand?"

"But, Dad, the whole point is to get her launched while Philippe's here, and he leaves tomorrow," objected Peter.

"I can't help that. It's disappointing, of course, but not half as disappointing as the loss of your boat would be, and very likely the loss of your own lives into the bargain! The very idea of attempting to launch a boat in a sea like that! I never heard such nonsense in my life!" With which he opened his paper with a crackle that showed, beyond any possible doubt, that the subject was closed.

The entrance of Mrs. Bevan with breakfast raised their spirits somewhat, for among the crisp rashers of bacon lay flat, round cakes of laverbread, rolled in oatmeal and fried until the green was lightly overlaid with a crust of golden brown.

But when the meal was over they wandered out to the boatshed and the vexing question of the name cropped up again. After days of wrangling and discussion they had finally narrowed the list to three names, but as each of the three considered his own selection the only possible choice it looked as though they would have to draw lots when the time for launching came. Peter had eventually decided that *Solan Goose* would be the perfect name. Robert stuck to his original *Wanderer*, while Stella, after agonies of indecision, had suddenly hit on *Spindrift*. Since Philippe was not one of the owners of the boat he was not really entitled to a choice, but whenever the subject came under discussion he slipped in his monotonous "*Evelyn Starr*" until somebody silenced him.

As the morning wore on the weather grew steadily worse outside and the tempers shorter indoors. For want of anything better to do they continued to argue over the name until Stella slammed out of the shed in exasperation. As a result she missed the moment when Peter had his splendid inspiration. However, they very soon called her back to share it.

"Peter's thought where we can launch the boat this evening!" announced Robert.

"This evening? But I thought Daddy said . . ." began Stella doubtfully.

"I don't see how he can possibly mind the salt marsh," said Peter.

"The marsh?" Stella was thoroughly puzzled.

"Yes, the marsh. You remember all those creeks where the coal boats used to come in years ago?"

"But those creeks are nothing but mud, there's hardly more than an inch of water in them now," objected Stella.

"Usually, yes," agreed Peter, "but it happens that tonight is the highest tide of the month—and incidentally one of the highest tides of the year into the bargain. Those big tides always fill the creeks, and quite often flood most of the marsh itself as well."

"Like that special tide we went down to see one evening last September," remembered Stella.

"That's right. And the beauty of it is that although it is, of course, sea water flowing into the creeks, the marsh itself is technically inland, sheltered all along its seaward edge by the long curve of the sand dunes. So I really don't see how Dad could possibly mind, do you? There couldn't be any danger there.

"The only snag in the whole plan is the time," he went on. "It says here in the tidetable that high water is just after seven. Add an hour for Summer Time, which makes it just after eight. That means that it will be getting dark, which is rather a pity. Not that it really matters, of course, the moon's just past the full now, so there'll be plenty of light. The only thing that really matters is to get Dad to agree."

Mr. Bevan never came home to lunch, so they were faced with long hours of uncertainty. They consulted their mother, but although she agreed that the marsh seemed safe enough, she insisted that nothing could be decided without their father's approval.

"Couldn't we phone him, just this once?" pleaded Stella.

"Certainly not, you know very well we never ring the office except in an emergency."

"I should have thought this could almost count as an emergency with Philippe going home so soon," muttered Robert; but his remark was ignored.

"Well at any rate we might as well get everything ready in the hope that he'll agree," said Peter. "We can get her onto the launching trolley and pull it outside in readiness now that the rain looks as if it is stopping at last."

"And we'll need a bottle of wine for the christening," put in Robert. "Have you got any wine we could use, Mum?"

"Only last year's elderberry. You may have some of that if you like."

"Elderberry," mused Peter. "The only thing is, mightn't it stain the varnish? You remember what it did to Uncle Alan's trousers? It might be wiser to use a white wine, perhaps."

"My dear boy!" laughed his mother. "You speak as though the house is stocked with wines to be had for the asking! Don't forget that wine is very expensive stuff."

"I have it—brandy! That's pale enough," he exclaimed. "Have you got any left over from the Christmas puddings?"

"I have a little, as it happens, but I really like to keep it in case of illness."

"But we'd only want a tiny bit," explained Peter, "just to say she's been properly christened with wine, you know. About an egg-cupful would be enough."

"Oh, if that's all you need, I can certainly spare you that," she said. "I'll find a small bottle to put it in."

The boys decided it would be wisest not to mention the launching until Mr. Bevan had looked through the afternoon mail in peace. Then it was Peter, rather red in the face, who brought up the subject.

Mr. Bevan was sceptical at first. "But those channels are practically dry," he objected, just as Stella had done.

"Not tonight," said Peter triumphantly. "There are some of the highest tides of the year this week, and the highest of all is at eight o'clock tonight. And the moon's only just past the full," he went on, "so the light shouldn't be too bad. Not that it's ever all that dark on the marsh, away from the trees and hills."

"Hmm, you seem to have it all worked out anyway," grunted his father. "Very well, go ahead, you can't do much worse than run aground on the marsh, whatever the state of the tide. But remember, you're to remain on the marsh, don't attempt to go anywhere near the dunes or the outlet to the sea. Is that clearly understood?"

"Oh yes, of course it is, and thanks, Dad," said Peter.

"Sorry I can't help you pull the boat down, it'll be a longish trek to the marsh, I'm afraid. But your mother and I have to go over to the Paynes' tonight, as you know."

"Oh we'll be all right, Dad, we've lifted her onto the trolley already. She'll be easy to handle with four of us on the job."

By late afternoon a watery sun was doing its best to break through the angry clouds that were still sweeping across the sky.

The salt marsh lay some distance from the village, so they set out at once, intending to give themselves plenty of time to prepare for the launching.

But although the boat was light, the trolley proved an awkward thing to pull against the wind. It kept jerking out of their grasp and ramming the hedge, or slewing across the road when they least expected it. As a result the distance seemed longer than ever before, and the sun was already low in the sky by the time they reached the lane leading down to the marsh. And here there was another unexpected hold-up.

"Look!" said Robert. "Dogs."

"And sheep, a large flock by the sound of it," added Peter. "Who on earth can be moving sheep at this time of day? It'll soon be dark."

"Well, here they come, anyway," observed Stella as the first white face rounded a bend in the lane below them.

"Lucky we weren't already down there with the boat, there'd never have been room for them and us," remarked Peter as the flock came flowing up the narrow lane towards them like a turbulent white river. Three black-and-white sheepdogs ran behind, darting excitedly up and down the steep banks as they herded the flock up the hill. Last of all came the farmer, a young man from the cottage at the top of the lane.

"Tide's going to be high tonight," he announced as he came abreast of them. "I reckon it's safest to drive this lot in from the marsh in case they might get caught."

"But wouldn't they come in on their own when they saw the water rising?" asked Robert.

"Ah, they would, of course; sheep aren't near so daft as people think. All the same, with the wind in this direction, I guess it might come in a good deal faster than usual, and higher, too, I shouldn't wonder. Besides, the way the water comes creeping up those gullies they could be cut off before they knew the tide was there. I've never forgotten the time when my poor old dad lost near a dozen sheep on this marsh when I was a kid. A high tide, and a following wind, that's all it was. But the damage was done before anyone realised what was happening. I learnt my lesson then, and I'm taking no chances now."

He had been eyeing the boat with interest as he spoke, and he now remarked, "Well you should have a grand night for your boating, anyway. 'Tisn't often you can use any sort of a boat down here, not since the channels silted up after they stopped the coal boats coming in.

"Ah well, I must be on my way and see to the gates, I suppose; that's the only thing my dogs can't do for me!" and with a laugh and a nod he strode on up the hill.

The lane was rough as well as narrow, and they had to manoeuvre the boat with the greatest care to avoid damaging her varnish against the high banks where sprawling brambles added a further hazard. Wind-bent hawthornes arched overhead, festooned in old-man's beard, turning the lane into a shadowed tunnel. By the time they reached the end of it the sun had set in a sullen glow, leaving the massed grey clouds flushed with angry red. Soon the last of the colour died away, and as they came to the stunted thistles that fringed the first creek, twilight stole over the marsh, lending an air of mystery to the scene.

"You know," said Stella suddenly, "if the boat is going to be launched in the dark I think she ought to have a special nightish sort of name. If only we could think of something we all liked, then we needn't draw lots after all."

"Not a bad idea," said Robert, "a night name ought to be something mysterious and exciting. How about *Shooting Star*?"

"Or *Night Hawk*," suggested Peter.

"I like *Evelyn Starr*," murmured Philippe monotonously, before anyone could stop him.

Stella stopped dead.

"I have it!" she shouted, waking an unexpected echo over the marsh, "really I have. Only please don't all say 'no' before you even think, because it's a good name, truly it is, and it's got a bit of everyone's suggestion; 'night' for Peter—well, almost night, anyway—and Robert's 'star' and even the *sound* of Philippe's *Evelyn Starr*. Actually, it was his saying that that really gave me the idea."

"Well, what is it, for goodness' sake?" demanded Robert impatiently.

"*Evening Star*," said Stella.

There was a momentary silence during which she scanned the three faces, anxiously trying to read their expressions in the failing light.

"Mm, not bad, not bad at all," said Peter.

"*Evening Star*," mused Robert. "Yes, that really is a good name, I must say."

Philippe surprised them all by remarking tranquilly, "I like that."

Stella said nothing, but she hugged herself with secret delight. For in addition to pleasing everyone, she had actually persuaded them to accept a name that was not only beautiful and romantic, but one that even included something of her own name, too. Wisely she decided not to point this out to anyone, except perhaps to Mummy, who would understand, and laugh with her in secret.

When they got out onto the marsh, they found the creeks already filling with water, while at the far side, under the dunes, the sea was beginning to steal in over the flat, low-lying land, although it was too dark to see this clearly.

It was not a marsh of reeds and rushes, the periodic inroads of the sea making it unsuitable for any but salt-loving plants. As a result it was carpeted with the transparent skeletons of sea pinks and a haze of blue sea lavender. A few adventurous daisies risked a wetting, their perky little faces standing out defiantly against the dark carpet of matted leaves that covered the mud. A straggling tide line of leaves and twigs wavered around the shallow pools, with little to remind one of the sea save the brittle shells of small dead crabs, bleached to a washed-out pink.

Leaving the boat at the edge of the marsh, Peter walked along the bank of the deepest channel, looking for a suitable spot for the launching.

"It looks all right here," he announced after a careful reconnaisance. "The bank is firm enough to bear the weight of the trolley, and there's a good, smooth slope of mud to slide her down as soon as the water's deep enough to float her; and that won't be long, judging by the rate it's coming in."

They stood together for a moment watching the steady rise of the water, then hurried back to fetch the boat, pulling the trolley along the bank to the selected spot.

Peter turned to Stella.

"You must do the actual naming, of course," he said, handing her the bottle. "It's usually done by a woman."

Stella had not expected this and was very thrilled to be chosen for such an honour.

"What do I have to do?" she asked anxiously.

"I should imagine the best plan will be for you to get into the boat. You might not be able to reach her from the bank once she begins to move. Luckily, you aren't heavy, so we should be able to manage all right with three of us to do the pushing."

"And what must I do then? Smash the bottle against her bow and say 'I name you *Evening Star*'?"

"Oh, surely she must also say, 'And may good fortune attend you and all who sail in you,' " added Robert.

"Yes, I believe she should say something of the sort," agreed Peter, but he spoke absently. From his next words it was evident what was troubling him—

"It's this business of breaking the bottle I don't like," he admitted. "I'm so afraid the broken glass will scratch the varnish."

"I hadn't thought of that," said Robert. "It easily might, especially as it will take a pretty hefty wallop to break that tough little bottle."

"I know," agreed Peter. "And yet there's the danger that it might not break at all if Stella was worrying about the varnish. So why shouldn't she just pour the brandy over the bow instead of actually breaking the bottle? After all, the important thing is for the boat to receive her name and the wine as she hits the water, isn't it?"

They all agreed that this was the wisest plan, and Stella loosened the bottle top in readiness.

While they had been talking, the channel had filled steadily and the water was now halfway up the muddy banks.

"Won't be long now," announced Peter. "Better start getting her off the trolley."

The three boys gripped the sides of the boat and slid her off the trolley, pulling her to the brink of the steep bank.

"Hop in now, Stella," commanded Peter.

Holding her bottle carefully, Stella climbed into the boat and crawled forward into the bow. Now that she was actually inside it, the boat seemed surprisingly small and frail. She took off the cap of the bottle and waited, her heart quickening with excitement. It was a solemn moment and the eerie half light added to the drama of the occasion.

"Ready?" called Peter.

"Yes," whispered Stella.

The boys gave the boat a mighty shove and she started to slither down the few feet of steep bank, gathering speed as she moved. She hit the water with a mighty splash and Stella, who had wondered if her voice would do what she wanted in the excitement, found herself shouting a good deal more loudly than she had intended—

"I name you *Evening Star,* and may good fortune attend you and all who sail in you!" In the same moment the heady smell of brandy rose about her as she sprinkled the contents of the bottle over the bow.

The boat tossed for a moment on the disturbed water, then the wave caused by her launching rippled away up the channel with a gradually diminishing sound, leaving the newly launched boat lying quietly against the muddy bank. Stella reached out and held her steady against the stump of an ancient mooring post, while the boys dragged the trolley back to the foot of the lane, well above the reach of any possible tide.

"Doesn't she look marvellous in the water?" exclaimed Robert on their return.

"She certainly looks all right," admitted Peter cautiously. "How does she ride, Stella?"

"She's perfect," breathed Stella ecstatically. She could still scarcely believe her luck in being the very first person afloat in this wonderful boat.

The others lowered themselves in carefully, the boat settling well down in the water under their added weight.

"She's still not touching bottom though," said Peter with satisfaction. "All the same, we'll need to feel our way along pretty cautiously to make sure we don't run aground. We'll have to work her along with an oar over the stern until we get clear of the channel, anyway. But I hope we'll be able to row once we get out onto the flooded part of the marsh itself."

He stood up as he spoke, dipping the blade of his oar into the water astern. They had not brought the rudder, and the centre-board was raised, since it was essential that the boat should draw as little as possible in these shallow waters.

Once Peter got the boat moving steadily, they drifted along in a silence broken only by the ripple of water under their bow. At first the steep sides of the gully cut off all view of the marsh, and there was nothing to see but a sparse fringe of straggling marsh sedges silhouetted against the rapidly darkening sky.

But soon the channel widened into what appeared to be a shallow inland sea. It was still necessary to keep to the unseen channel however, as the water was no more than an inch or two deep on either side. Stella could just make out the white shapes of daisy heads, up to their necks in water, looking for all the world like miniature water lilies, while their buds could be seen submerged below the surface. Leaning closer she saw glistening bubbles imprisoned among the leaves in an under-water world which reminded her of the delicate Venetian flowers in the depths of the old glass paperweight on her mother's desk at home.

"Funny stuff, mud," observed Robert musingly. "You'd expect it to smell horrible, but it doesn't, you know, not this mud, anyhow, it's got a most exciting smell," and he sniffed the salty tang appreciatively. Nobody troubled to reply, nor did he expect an answer; it was one of those companionable silences in which you only spoke if you felt like it, without worrying whether anyone listened or not.

As they drifted along, Stella noticed several unfortunate insects floundering helplessly in the water that had flowed so unexpectedly over their little world. There were ladybirds and beetles, and a yellow-banded caterpillar reaching out from the last dry petal on a plant of drowned sea rocket. There was also a small snail sailing past in mute surprise on a floating feather. She rescued as many of these as she could reach, dropping them quietly into the bow of the boat, to be put ashore when next they touched dry land. She decided to say nothing about this strange little party of refugees, fearing the scorn of her brothers.

"Look!" cried Philippe, speaking for the first time. "There is the evening star, the real one, in the sky, come out perhaps to welcome her new sister!"

And there, sure enough, was the first star twinkling down through the ragged clouds, its small light reflected in the vastness of the flooded marsh.

It was now so dark that the encircling dunes appeared as no more than a dim smudge bordering the pale sheet of water. Sweet liquid calls of water fowl sounded now and again; it was too dark to see the birds themselves, but occasional plops and splashings betrayed their whereabouts.

Stella leant over the bow of the boat, picturing herself as

the figurehead of the newly launched vessel. She had seldom known such utter peace, and she wished this maiden voyage might go on forever. But all too soon Peter broke into her reverie, asking her to pass the torch which he flashed onto the face of his watch.

"I was afraid of it," he said regretfully. "It's time to be turning back."

"Oh, Peter, need we?" she implored.

"Afraid so. It's just about high water now, and it'll take us a good while to get back to our starting point. After all, it wouldn't be funny to get stranded out here on an ebbing tide and have to drag the *Evening Star* home across acres of slippery mud."

It was not at all easy to locate the channel on the return journey, as there were few landmarks to go by, one tuft of grass looking very much like another. They ran aground so frequently that Peter decided to put a lookout in the bow, using the second oar to test for depth as they went along, and fend off as necessary. Philippe was chosen for this job since he was lighter than Robert, and also more accustomed to handling oars.

"All our landmarks seem to have shrunk since we passed them on the way out," observed Stella.

"I know," said Robert, "and lots of the little ones have vanished completely. So the water must still be rising."

"Yes, but once it starts to ebb it will go down pretty fast, you know," Peter reminded him.

Even the islands of slightly higher ground had dwindled, and were now little more than sparse patches of greenery standing a couple of inches above the water.

"Whatever's that?" cried Stella suddenly, pointing to one of these patches. Above the thin line of grass and sea lavender

a dim white blur could be seen, like a solid, low-lying cloud.

"What on earth can it be?" wondered Robert, trying to focus his eyes in the dim light.

They drifted closer.

"It's a sheep!" exclaimed Peter suddenly.

"A sheep? Oh, Peter, how awful, it must have got marooned," cried Stella in an agonized tone.

"That farmer must have missed one, after all," said Peter. "Poor thing, it's done its best, making for the highest patch of ground in reach. But I'm afraid it looks as though even that will soon be under water."

"Can sheep swim?" asked Robert.

"The farmer said his father's lot were drowned, so I shouldn't imagine they swim very well," replied Peter. "Probably get weighed down by their heavy fleece. Here, Philippe, try for depth your end and see if it's deep enough for us to get across and rescue her."

Philippe probed with the oar and they decided it might just be possible to make their way across the intervening stretch of water.

"If only it doesn't start to ebb too quickly," muttered Robert anxiously.

"If it ebbs she'll be all right provided she stays where she is," Peter reminded him. "I'm worried about what will happen if the water rises another inch or two; it's up to the tops of her legs already."

As they got nearer they saw the water beginning to creep up around the animal's sides. She made no sound or movement, merely standing there staring at them helplessly.

"I'm only afraid she may suddenly try to get away when we come near," muttered Peter in an undertone.

His fears were justified; the poor creature did make one frantic effort to escape, but the waterlogged ground on which she stood was so insecure that she merely sank more deeply into the mud, causing the water to lap around her shoulders.

"Quick! Quick! Oh hurry, please!" whispered Stella, quite unaware that she had spoken at all.

"We'll surely never get her into the boat?" asked Robert hesitantly.

"Oh, no," said Peter, "I doubt we could lift her over the side without capsizing. Besides, I think the weight of a large water-logged sheep added to our present boatload would just about sink us anyway. Or if we didn't sink we'd certainly find ourselves touching bottom in this shallow water."

As it happened, they touched bottom before they even reached the sheep, although bottom, in this case, consisted of no more than the tops of drowned bushes over which they scraped uncomfortably. Peter groaned inwardly, thinking of the varnish. However, he shipped his oar, and grabbing the stoutest twigs in reach, pulled the boat into all that was left of the so-called island.

"Now, Stella, be ready to catch her before she starts to struggle again," he ordered.

Stella leant over the side and seized a handful of sopping wet fleece. The creature proved to be a full-grown lamb and so had not been shorn. As a result her thick wool was soaking up the water like a sponge.

"I don't believe she could possibly swim with all this weight," remarked Robert, gripping the wet fleece himself. "It'd be like us trying to swim in layers of heavy woollen sweaters."

"Well, she'll have to do her best," said Peter. "What you and Stella must do is to hold her head above water while Philippe and I back out of these beastly bushes. Whatever you do, don't let go, either of you, or she really might go under."

He and Philippe drove their oars into the yielding thicket, managing to get just enough purchase to push off into clear water. Robert and Stella held the sheep's head firmly between them. In addition Robert gripped a handful of fleece in the middle of the animal's back. With their help she managed to flounder along beside the boat, sometimes swimming and sometimes striking such temporary footholds as came within reach of her thrashing hoofs. It was all they could do to keep her head above water.

"You're going to be all right, we're rescuing you," Stella assured her soothingly, worried by the glazed look in the animal's rolling eyes.

The next twenty minutes seemed like hours, and none of the four was ever to forget that voyage. To counterbalance the weight of the sheep and her two supporters, Peter and Philippe had to stand together on the opposite side of the boat, using every ounce of their combined strength to keep her moving at all. Where the water was deep they encountered nothing worse than submerged bushes, but elsewhere their oars skidded and stuck, caught in the mud of unexpected shallows. Eventually they regained the channel. But although the water was deeper here, their difficulties increased, for the ebbing tide was against them now, and running out at a great rate.

Meanwhile Robert and Stella were having an alarming time with the sheep, which suddenly appeared to have given up all hope. She had ceased to try to swim or struggle, merely floating along beside the boat looking so resigned that Stella was sure she was dying, if not already dead. Their arms ached with the effort of keeping her nostrils clear of the water, and at the same time supporting her sagging body. Thinking it over afterwards they often wondered how they ever got to their destination.

By the time they reached the point at which they had

launched the boat the tide had ebbed so far that there was scarcely enough water left in the channel to float her at all. Peter leapt ashore and fastened the painter to the broken mooring post that Stella had used at the launching.

As soon as the boat was secured they were able to concentrate their united efforts on the sheep. The poor creature certainly needed all their help as she was by this time far too exhausted to do anything for herself.

The recent tide had made the banks of mud too slippery to climb; the only possible way to get out of the creek was to wade to a point upstream where the banks were low enough to enable them to haul the stumbling animal ashore.

"What now?" demanded Robert when they reached the top.

"Well, we'll obviously have to get her up to the farm," replied Peter without much enthusiasm.

"Oh, poor thing, she doesn't look fit to walk any farther," said Stella pityingly. "I'm so afraid she might have a heart attack or something." As she said these words a sudden idea occurred to her.

"Oh, I wonder!" she exclaimed. "There just might be a few drops of brandy left in the bottom of the bottle; that would revive her, wouldn't it?"

"Oh, look here, you don't want to waste time wading all the way back to the boat, it's late enough as it is," expostulated Peter, who was now impatient to get the business over as quickly as possible, and concentrate on the job of hauling the boat home.

"But I needn't wade; without the sheep I can go along the bank. If you start up the hill with her I'll soon catch up with you. Can you see your way all right if I borrow the torch?"

When she got back to the boat, she was relieved to find a

good half inch of brandy in the bottom of the bottle. While there she also seized the opportunity to put her refugees ashore before hurrying after the others whose voices could be heard halfway up the lane.

"She's getting awfully tottery," admitted Robert in a worried tone as she joined them. "I do hope she's not going to pass out on us after all."

"Let's try her with the brandy, there was a bit left," said Stella, her fingers trembling in her anxiety to unscrew the bottle quickly.

It was a desperately difficult business forcing the sheep's jaws open, and even harder to pour the brandy down her throat without losing the few precious drops. But the dose, or possibly the way in which it was given, had an immediate effect.

"Wow!" yelled Robert as the sheep surged forward unexpectedly. "I hope she's not going to escape from us now!"

"Call the farmer, somebody!" shouted Peter, straddling the lane with outstretched arms in case the sheep should suddenly decide to double back to the marsh.

Stella raced up the lane and knocked on the cottage door. The farmer opened it himself.

"Oh, please, can you come!" she panted. "One of the sheep got caught by the tide but we saved her. The others have got her outside."

Shutting the door on two of his dogs the farmer called to the third and they hurried out to join the group in the lane.

"Oh, she'll soon come now," he assured them. "Only let her dry off and she'll be a different creature. My! But she wouldn't have lasted long if you'd not rescued her! It was a high old tide right enough." Then, signing to the dog to remain at heel, he turned to guide the sheep up the rough track, talking to her in soothing tones as he urged her along with a firm, reassuring hand—

"Come up now, girl, come up with you," he encouraged, "that's the way, steady now, steady . . ."

As she followed the boys down the lane to the boat Stella remarked thoughtfully—

"D'you realise something? The *Evening Star* has actually saved a life on her maiden voyage!"

Chapter 7

NEXT DAY old Martha was buried. It was also the day for Philippe's return to France.

"Oh, Philippe, I wish you needn't go!" sighed Stella. "We've still got quite a bit of the holidays left, and now that the storm is dying down we'll be able to sail *Evening Star* right here in the bay in a day or two—oh, I do wish you could stay for that!"

"I wish also," replied Philippe, "and, too, I wish we could find out how it can be arranged for Sammy and his creatures to stay in the shore cottage. I wanted to see what the Colonel meant about *Evelyn Starr* holding Sam's security in the hollow of her hand."

"Actually that bit really is only a sort of expression, as Peter said," she explained. "It just means she's a kind of good-luck mascot, in a way."

But Philippe shrugged away this suggestion with scorn.

"I do not think," he said decidedly. "He meant something more than just good luck or Martha would not have remembered it all these years. If only I could go and look for myself . . . but of course!" he exclaimed, looking up in sudden excitement. "We can go down there and look at it now—the funeral must be over by this time, and my bus doesn't leave for over an hour, so there'll just be time if we are quick. Come on!" In a moment he was out of the gate and racing down through the village with Stella at his heels.

But when they got to the cottage they found people still about. The village women had arranged to come in turns to look after Sammy until his future was decided. Today it was the turn of deaf old Mrs. Jones who was already in the little kitchen, taking over from a neighbour who had lingered for a chat.

Sammy himself was sitting outside in the sunshine, arranging shells on the bench beneath the figurehead. Stella had secretly dreaded the moment of meeting him again, but was relieved to find him just as usual, humming to himself as though nothing had happened.

"Come and look what I found on the tide!" he called when he caught sight of her peering over the wall, and leaving his shells she pounced on a much-discoloured golf ball and held it out for her to admire.

"But Cawdaw likes it, too," he said with his shy, sideways smile. "I must keep it hidden safe or he will steal it away."

Stella was pleased to see that he now accepted Philippe as naturally as he accepted the rest of her family, making no attempt to slide indoors when they joined him under the figurehead.

They were bending over the shells on the bench when a sudden footstep made them turn. A brisk, thickset man was rounding the corner of the cottage from the narrow strip of garden that backed onto the hill behind.

"Hah! Sammy!" he shouted in an unnecessarily loud and jovial tone; then, seeing that Sam had visitors he added somewhat uncertainly: "Ah yes, and young Miss . . . er . . . er . . . Sheila Bevan, isn't it?"

"Stella," she corrected, smiling politely. "And this is our friend Philippe Griveau, Mr. Griffiths."

Philippe gave a stiff little bow, but a dangerous light leapt into his eyes as he guessed what brought Mr. Griffiths to the shore cottage at this particular time.

It was evident, however, that Mr. Griffiths had no intention of mentioning the purpose of his visit while they were there, and almost at once he went indoors where he could be heard trying to make conversation with Mrs. Jones, although her deafness made this difficult.

Philippe turned his attention to the figurehead, climbing up on the bench among the shells.

"That's *Evelyn Starr*, she's my figurehead," said Sammy proudly. But Philippe was too preoccupied to spare him much attention. His head was now on a level with the figure's shoulders, and he was able to examine the heavily ringed hand half buried among the ruffles of her bodice.

"There is not much of a hollow at all," he remarked. "These ruffles must be part of the disguise, I expect. But I can't feel anything even when I do get my finger inside."

"But, Philippe, I told you, that bit about the hollow of her hand is only a saying, really it is," persisted Stella. "It must be something more than that we have to look for."

Philippe made no reply to this. He merely raised himself on tiptoe and went on probing until he became aware of a figure in the doorway, and looked round to find Mr. Griffiths watching him curiously. Stella saw him too, and moving a pace nearer the bench, murmured under her breath, "I think we'd better be going, Philippe, we can't do much with him watching us like that. And however long we stay, he's obviously determined to stay longer still."

They trailed back across the beach in a dejected frame of mind, and it was a sombre little party that eventually set out to catch the bus.

"If only you had even one more day we might all have gone for a sail," said Robert as they settled into the four front seats of the bus and waved good-bye to Mrs. Bevan. She had remained behind, anxious to call on Sammy and learn the reason for Mr. Griffiths' visit if she could.

On the way to the station, Peter suggested calling at Captain Morgan's Store for a couple of cleats and the buoyancy bags they had ordered for the boat. Philippe stood watching enviously as these tantalizing purchases were made. He cheered up, however, when they called at the chemist's next door and found that his photographs were ready.

"Some good ones of the boat being varnished, and one of her on the trolley, too," he murmured, thumbing through them rapidly as he shuffled his way along the crowded pavement. "Oh, and some super ones of *Evelyn Starr*, look at this! And this one's even better."

They passed the prints from hand to hand until it dawned on Peter that they were in danger of missing the train. As a result they rushed into the station in a final breathless flurry, and Philippe tumbled into the train as the doors were closing. He dumped his rucksack in the corridor and hung out of the window as the guard's whistle shrilled.

"I'll write and tell you what happens about Sammy," promised Stella.

"Maybe *Evelyn Starr* will help him even now," he called as the train began to move.

"You know we're going to miss old Philippe," remarked Robert as they made their way towards the exit. "Funny thing, he's quieter than any of us, but there's something about him we are going to miss a lot. We don't even seem to argue so much when he's around."

"I know, and I was looking forward to sailing with him, he'd have been a terrific help," said Peter.

Stella said nothing; she knew she was going to miss him more than anyone.

When they got off the bus in the village they met their mother coming up from the beach. She looked worried and Stella ran to meet her.

"Oh, Mum, it's Sammy, isn't it?" she cried. "Is it bad news?"

"I'm afraid it is. I've been talking to Mr. Griffiths and it looks as though he really is putting the shore cottage up for sale."

"But, Mummy, what about Sammy and all his creatures, what'll happen to them all?"

"I know," sighed Mrs. Bevan, "I tried to discuss alternatives, explaining that poor old Sammy would be quite lost without his creatures."

"And what did he say to that?" demanded Robert.

"I'm afraid I just couldn't make him see the point at all. He's determined to believe what he wants to believe, and has managed to persuade himself that Sammy will be much better off in the hostel. I begin to see what people mean when they say he's hard. I don't doubt he intends to use the money from the sale of the cottage for the good of the estate as a whole, that is always his way. Nevertheless, I don't feel it is justified in this particular case."

"I suppose there'd be absolutely no chance of the hostel allowing him even one of his creatures, the guillemot, say, or Willie?" ventured Robert. But he spoke without much hope.

"Oh, no, I'm afraid that would be out of the question," said his mother.

"But what about Sammy himself, isn't he absolutely frantic?" demanded Stella.

"To tell the truth I doubt he's actually taken it in at all, he seems perfectly happy whenever the hostel is mentioned, then goes straight on to talk of the fish he'll catch for Ellygug, which shows that he simply hasn't realised that he won't be able to go fishing from the hostel. Nor will he have the guillemot to feed, of course." She sighed and went on angrily: "And the infuriating part of it is that Mr. Griffiths takes Sammy at face value, only too pleased to believe that he will be as happy at the hostel as he is when he's told about it now. I can't seem to make him see that Sammy just doesn't understand what is being planned. Dear old Colonel Griffiths would have managed things differently, I know; he'd have seen that Sammy lived out the remainder of his days in the shore cottage."

"D'you think he just might let him stay if I promised to go in after school every evening and get Sammy's tea and dust around a bit? I easily could," said Stella.

Her mother smiled but shook her head.

"Something of the sort has already been suggested; several of the women living at the lower end of the village near the shore have said they'd gladly work out some sort of a schedule between them, as they have been doing all this week, of course."

"That's because everyone's so fond of Sammy, nobody'll want him to go out of the village," said Stella.

"I know," said her mother sadly, "and it seems such a little thing to ask. All that's necessary is for someone to look in once or twice a day to make sure he's all right, and maybe do a bit of cooking and cleaning, as they'd all be glad to do. And Sam's not one to mind being on his own. It would never occur to him to feel lonely, provided he'd got his creatures round him for company. No, I'm afraid the truth of it is Mr. Griffiths knows he'll get an excellent price for the cottage and is glad of an excuse to sell it. But come along now, we can't stand talking here all the afternoon, let's go in and see about a meal."

In the days following Philippe's departure Stella would have felt very much alone if it hadn't been for the *Evening Star*. But as it was, she was kept so constantly busy on the boat that there was little time to think about anything else. And even when she got to bed at night, she found herself going over all the knots the boys were teaching her.

First of all they rigged the boat, and as the weather was fine they did this out of doors, pulling her round to the sheltered side of the house.

"But even here there's a bit of wind," observed Peter. "The book says she must stand head to wind, so we'll need to swing her round a bit. There—I should think that's about right."

They attached the foresail first, then spread the mainsail on the lawn.

"Look, Stella, you might be fitting these battens into the pockets along the edge of the sail, while Robert and I fix the boom," suggested Peter.

It soon turned out that there were many jobs where Stella's quick, neat fingers were a help, and she herself was delighted to find ropes and sails much easier to understand than the complicated building of the hull. She proved so quick and helpful that even Robert was impressed.

The storm eventually blew itself out, to be followed by a spell of calm sunny weather. At last they were able to take the boat down to their own beach and launch her on the ebbing tide.

"We'll have to sail her pretty gently at first," warned Peter as they got under way. "The book says we must avoid putting any strain on the sails until they are fully stretched."

"Oh dear, how long will that take?" demanded Robert, always the impatient one.

Stella, on the other hand, was content with any speed just so long as they were afloat, and as she watched the shore recede she was completely happy.

The weather continued calm and bright, with just enough breeze to enable the boys to learn to handle the boat under ideal conditions. Stella soon learned to take certain jobs as her own, becoming very handy at working the centreboard and coiling ropes and making sure that the rowlocks were in place when they were needed.

As a result the long days slipped happily by and it was only when they came in from the sea that they remembered Sammy's troubles. These troubles loomed very large, indeed, when a sale notice appeared on the gate of the shore cottage and people began to troop down through the sand dunes to inspect it.

To Stella's surprise she did not hear from Philippe. Her mother had an appreciative little letter of thanks written as soon as he reached home, and in it he mentioned that he would be writing to Stella soon. But although she watched the post from day to day, no letter came.

The day for the sale of Sammy's cottage drew nearer and the Bevans began to realise that this unbelievable thing was really about to happen.

"Poor old Sammy, not much more than a week now," said Robert soberly.

It was a clear evening, too clear; across, the Channel Ilfracombe glowed in a blaze of light, while lighthouses winked around the coast as far as Hartland Point—a sure sign that a change of weather was on the way. But for the moment it was still and mild and they sat by the open window, reluctant to draw the curtains on the soft September dusk. Stella sighed as she followed the direction of Robert's gaze and picked out the dim point of light that marked Sammy's little window on the shore.

"Not much hope of a reprieve for him now," said Peter, "so we'd really better be making our own plans, I suppose." He reached for his pen and a notebook that lay on the table, remarking in a businesslike tone—

"Now then, we'll obviously have to work out a timetable amongst ourselves and take it in turns to put out food and water for Sammy's creatures. It's no use attempting to shut any of them up in cages, they've been used to freedom all this while and would only pine if we tried to cage them now. So the best we can do is to feed them just as Sam has done, and with luck I suppose they may eventually go back to their wild state. Anyway, as far as I can see that's the best we can hope to do for them."

"Better make us a copy of the timetable each," suggested Robert, settling down with his elbows on the table.

"Good idea," said Stella. "Then we can pin them up on our bedroom walls where we'll be sure to see them every day. Well, for a start, of course, there's fish for Ellygug, all day long . . ."

"And Willie, any idea what he eats?" asked Robert.

"Biscuits, nuts, cake, he seems to eat almost anything. Oh, but how will we keep him warm?" cried Stella. "I'm so afraid he'll be cold and lonely out of Sammy's pocket."

"I should imagine the hedgehog can fend for itself, anyway," mused Peter. "But there's Cawdaw, of course, now I wonder what we'll need for him?"

The list grew and the details took so long to arrange that the dusk gave place to darkness before they had done.

Next day the weather worsened again, and high winds made

it clear that the *Evening Star* would not be able to put to sea again for a day or two. After the first disappointment the boys vanished into the shed, and were soon so busy preparing a lighting board to be used on the trolley at night that the weather was forgotten.

But Stella found this a thoroughly boring job and she sulked about at a loose end, driving her mother distracted.

"I wish that wretched boy would write," she complained to her husband.

The only reminder Stella had of Philippe was the arrival of a couple of Breton onion boys in the village. They were riding bicycles slung with heavy strings of onions which they hawked from door to door. Stella watched listlessly as her mother bought a couple of strings from the boy who called at their own back door. He was a tall fellow of eighteen or so, and he stared about the kitchen with lively curiosity, showing such marked interest in Stella herself that she was glad of the excuse to take the onions from her mother and hurry out of the room to hang them in the larder. She had an idea that if her mother had not been there he would have tried to speak to her, although it was clear from his attempt at conversation with Mrs. Bevan that he scarcely understood a word of English.

"Philippe says lots of those onion johnnies come from Roscoff where his uncle lives," she observed when the boy had cycled off to join his companion up the road.

"Oddly enough, he reminded me of Philippe," remarked her mother. "Older, of course, and taller, but the same sort of look about him somehow. It's a Breton type, I suppose."

Chapter 8

THERE was still a big sea running the following morning, and the boys resigned themselves to another day's work in the shed. After lunch, for want of anything better to do, Stella went down to the shore cottage to have a further word with Sammy about the creatures that would so soon be her responsibility.

She found him sitting in the doorway with Ellygug. Moving slowly forward she held out her hand to the bird, which showed no fear.

"I think he's really beginning to know me," she said hopefully.

"Ah, knows you, that's right," agreed Sammy.

A gust of wind chose this moment to swirl around the cottage, ruffling the guillemot's feathers until he squawked with annoyance.

"Still a good deal of wind," remarked Stella, more to herself than to Sammy. "I wonder how soon we'll be able to sail again."

She glanced out to where the waves were flinging up a wall of spray around Long Holm, which was surrounded now by the high tide. As she watched she fancied just for an instant that she saw a plume of smoke rise from the seaward end of the island. It mingled at once with the high-flung spray, and she was beginning to think she must have imagined it when she saw what appeared to be another puff. But this, too, was snatched away by the wind before she could be certain.

"Look, Sammy! Isn't that smoke out on the end of Long Holm?" she exclaimed, pointing towards the rocks.

Sammy followed her gaze without interest.

"There it is again—surely it's smoke, Sam?" she insisted.

"Smoke?" echoed Sammy absently, smoothing the guillemot's feathers.

"But, Sammy, how can it be? I mean, this isn't the weather for picnics, and anyway, it's high tide, who could be out there now?"

"Maybe somebody's lit a fire," suggested Sammy unhelpfully.

"But why? That's what I want to know. Who'd be out there on such a beastly day when they can't get away for four whole hours? Don't you see what I mean? Nobody ever goes there except on sunny days, and then only when the tide is low. Even I wouldn't want to be out there on a miserable day like this."

"Maybe it isn't a fire," said poor, bewildered Sammy, doing his best to say whatever it was she wanted him to say. She scarcely heard him; she was still staring at the island, trying to argue it out with herself—

"After all," she reasoned, "if somebody did get caught by the tide, and lighted a fire as a signal for help, they'd be there on the highest part of the island, waving like mad to attract attention."

But there was nobody waving anywhere, nor did she see a further sign of smoke, nothing except the wind-tossed spray rising above the island. She began to wonder if it could have been a trick of light on the flying spindrift. Nevertheless a niggling doubt nagged at her all the way home, and she kept stopping to look back again at the island, determined to go out there herself as soon as the tide went down. After tea she slipped out of the house again and ran down through the dunes to the bay.

Although there was still a high wind, the sun had struggled through the clouds and the beach was no longer deserted. Holiday-makers were beginning to pour out from caravans and cars and settle in groups along the shore with picnic suppers, making the most of the evening sunshine.

The tide was falling rapidly and the full length of the Long Holm causeway was uncovered. Stella hurried towards it, noticing that a family was already picking its way across the wet rocks ahead of her. The Holm was always a favourite objective at low tide, and people loved to picnic on Peter's and Robert's rough green lawns when they became accessible. Very few troubled to clamber out over the difficult rocks that led to her own "island," and she was relieved to see that nobody appeared to be out there now, although the rocks dividing it from Robert's cowrie beach must have been clear of the tide for a good hour already.

As she neared the end of her scramble, she slowed down, wondering for the first time what she was going to feel like if she really did find somebody on her island, possibly even in the cave itself. She hesitated for a moment, glancing back at the group on Robert's lawn, and actually found herself wishing they were just a little nearer, and wondering if they would hear if she called for help.

Then, pushing such nonsense out of her head, she scrambled to the top of the highest spur of her island and jumped down onto the ledge that ran across its seaward face. Her heart thumped uncomfortably and she was almost afraid to breathe as she edged towards the cave. When she got there it was empty.

She was crouching in the entrance, not quite sure whether to be relieved or disappointed, when suddenly she did see something. Just beyond the cave the remains of a fire smoul-

dered in a sheltered dip on the ledge. Stooping to see if the blackened rocks were warm she discovered charred ends of driftwood and burnt cork lying in a bed of ash that stirred and lifted in the teasing wind. In another hour it would all be blown away. It was evident that the fire itself had not been out very long.

Suddenly she was frightened, and scrambling up the steep slope she ran back over the rocks towards the reassuring mound of Robert's island. For once in her life she was thankful to see it a-sprawl with a nice, comfortable, ordinary sort of family.

For some strange reason Stella decided not to tell anyone about her discovery. But she spent so much time staring out towards the Holm that Robert became suspicious.

"You seem mighty interested in Long Holm all of a sudden," he observed. "What's up?"

"Oh, nothing," said Stella airily, turning away from the window. She could not have explained herself why she was so reluctant to share her secret. She supposed it was because it belonged to her island, making it very much her own private adventure.

She went to bed still puzzling over the mystery. For a mystery it undoubtedly was. It was clear that someone had lighted a fire on Long Holm at a time when it was cut off from the mainland by high tide. And on a morning of storm, moreover, the sort of morning on which no one could possibly choose to picnic there for pleasure. But who ever went out to Long Holm for anything else? And yet as soon as the tide went down and the sun came out, making the place attractive, this mysterious person vanished without a trace.

Before going to sleep she slipped out of bed for one last look. But the Holm lay dark and secret under the early stars.

Beyond the rocks a small light blinked spasmodically as the bell buoy plunged and rolled in the tumbled sea. There was no light to be seen on the Holm itself and she got back into bed still wondering, falling asleep to the sound of the wind rumbling around the house.

Her bedroom window clattered and banged throughout the night, and yet when a pebble hit the glass in the small hours of the morning the tiny "ping" jerked her awake in an instant. Before she had time to get out of bed the pebble was followed by an empty snail shell, which hit the pane with a totally different sound. She shot out of bed and darted across to the window to look out.

It was too dark to see the details of the garden, but she could just make out a shadowy figure standing against the darkness of the hedge. Whoever it was could evidently see her dim white shape at the window, for as she appeared it waved both arms and leapt into the air in silent greeting. Something in the movement was familiar, and she opened the window wider and leant out. The figure stepped out from the shadow of the hedge and stood on the lawn beneath her.

"Philippe!" she gasped.

"Sh!" he warned, gesticulating frantically to silence her.

This was altogether too much for anyone to expect. Snatching up her dressing gown she dragged it on. There was no time to bother with slippers—anyway it was easier to be quiet without them. She managed to open her door without its usual squeak, and creeping out she tiptoed along the landing and down the stairs.

The front door was directly under her parents' window so she went through to the kitchen and opened the back door instead. Philippe was waiting on the doorstep and slipped in like a

shadow. The first thing he did was to dart across to the electric switch and turn off the light she had just switched on.

"Safer," he whispered. "I'll draw the curtains first and then we can switch it on again. You see somebody might wake up and see the light shining across the path and come downstairs to see what's going on."

"But, Philippe, what is going on? And why is it all so secret?" she demanded as he pulled the curtains carefully.

"I tell you everything in a minute," he promised, flopping down on the nearest chair. "But before I tell, could you please give me something to eat, I am so hungry. But you must not give me any food your mother will miss, you understand."

"But why in the world?" expostulated Stella. "Mummy would want you to have whatever's in the larder, you know she would. She'd never care what's missing."

"Yes, but you see nobody must discover I am here."

"Not even the boys?"

"Better not."

"But why?" she persisted, flattered to be the only one entrusted with such a secret, but bewildered nonetheless. "Everybody loves having you here, surely you know that? They'd all be simply thrilled to know that you'd come back."

"Yes, but they would be sure to tell my parents—grown-up people do that sort of thing—and my papa would not be thrilled at all, he'd make me go home at once before I had a chance to look at *Evelyn Starr.*"

Stella could scarcely contain her curiosity, but she had enough sense to see that the boy was really tired and hungry. So, keeping back her questions, she went to see what she could collect in the way of food. As the larder had no curtain she borrowed his torch.

"I've cut little bits off lots of things," she explained when she returned. "It shows much less than taking big helpings from a few. I do hope it will be enough. Anyway I can get heaps more bread without it showing at all."

A happy grin spread over Philippe's face.

"That looks better than half-cooked laverbread and winkles." he remarked, pulling the nearest plate towards him.

Stella had collected a good haul: a slice of meat pie, two cold sausages, two tomatoes, thin slices of three different kinds of cake and a tablespoonful of custard. There was also an apple and three small pears. For drink she brought a glass of milk.

Phillippe fell on the food as though he hadn't eaten for a week, and he ate without speaking until nothing was left but a couple of pears.

"I keep these for another time, please," he said, dropping them into his pocket. "And now we must wash these dishes or your mother will ask questions in the morning." He carried the plates, glass, and knives to the sink where he rinsed them quietly under the hot tap. Then he returned for the cores of the apple, and pear, and was not satisfied until every crumb and tomato top was swept away, and the table left as clean and bare as they had found it. Only then was he ready to talk.

"Now I will tell you," he began, leaning back against the draining board. "You see when I got home and looked again at my snapshots of *Evelyn Starr* I saw where we have never looked. It was no good to write it to you in a letter because the strike might make it come too late, just like my mother's letter. So I have to come myself. And I have to come very quick before the shore cottage can be sold and Sammy sent away."

"But why does it all have to be such a secret?" puzzled Stella.

"Because of my father. He would never permit me to come here again so soon. He would insist that if anyone is to come it must be Marie-Thérèse. Her ankle is well again, you see, and Marie-Thérèse is very special with Papa."

"Yet you have come . . ." began Stella, more confused than ever.

Philippe grinned.

"I come over in my uncle's boat with the onion boys!" he explained. "But my father does not know, and my uncle, he does not know either! My cousin Yves hid me under the onions!"

"A stowaway!" breathed Stella admiringly.

"Ah so, of course, that is the word, a stowaway," repeated Philippe laughing. "But I think I shall smell of onions all my life! Can you smell them, too?"

"Why yes, now I come to think of it I can. But go on, what happened next?"

"Well there were several boats from Roscoff, all for different British ports. My uncle came up the Bristol Channel to Barry—we hoped he might go to Swansea or Port Talbot because that would have been better for me to get here. Yves and I came by train from Barry and got bicycles by hire to come out here from the station. And we have a big piece of luck. The boat damaged her propeller coming into harbour in the gale, so she will have to wait in dock till Friday for repairs. So we have a good lot of days."

"Have you just arrived in the village now, in the middle of the night?" asked Stella.

"No, we came the day before yesterday. That was Yves who sold onions to your mother at the back door."

"Why, Mummy said he was just like you!" she interrupted,

and then in response to his warning gesture she went on in a quieter voice—

"Oh, I've just thought of something! Was he trying to give me a message from you by any chance? He looked as though he might have been."

"Yes, but it does not matter now I have come here myself. But now listen, please. *Michelle*, that is the name of my uncle's boat, will be in dock until Friday when she sails on the morning tide. So I will have to get back to Barry in time to be a stowaway before she sails. Yves will be keeping a lookout for me and will tell me when it is safe to go on board. Only it will not be so easy to hide this time without the onions. But anyway, I have now got three days here to do the job."

"What job?" she began, but Philippe held up a hand for silence.

"A moment, please," he begged. "I tell you the plan first and then we talk. Now I have the money we got for the onions we sold. I will pay Yves back in francs when we get home in Brittany, but I need English money now, you understand, to buy food while I am here. And that is where I need your help. You see, I cannot go to the village shops, Mrs. Eynon and old Hughie would remember me at once. So if I give you the money, can you buy food for me? Not all at once because I have nowhere to keep it, but if you could buy enough for one day at a time I can come and fetch it from you every night. Or we might arrange somewhere for you to hide it, perhaps. Do you think you could do that?"

Stella's eyes shone with excitement.

"Why, Philippe, it'll be just like hiding an escaped Royalist from Cromwell's men!" she whispered. It was easier to remember to whisper now there was the thrill of a real conspiracy.

"O.K., then, here's the money," he said, and plunging his hands into his pockets he brought out handfuls of loose change, mainly coppers, which he heaped into her cupped hands. Before she had time for so much as a question he lifted a corner of the curtain and looked out.

"It's beginning to get light already," he announced. "I must go at once, I've a lot to do before people are up and about. I don't want anyone to recognise me now. It will be difficult enough to choose a safe moment to cross between the tides in daylight without being seen."

"To cross? Where? And what in the world have the tides to do with it?" she whispered, following him to the door.

Philippe stopped and faced her.

"Mind you, don't let this out to anyone," he warned her in an undertone. "You see I'm hiding in your cave on Long Holm."

"My cave! Oh Philippe it really is exactly like helping a fugitive to escape! Oh! I've just remembered something. Was it you who lighted a fire out on the Holm yesterday?"

"Yes," he replied. "But it was not easy. I had to be careful not to be seen. I hoped nobody would see the smoke with all that spray, especially as there did not seem to be anybody on the beach. But I am only safe on the island when the tide is high, of course. It would not be good for someone to walk out there and find me."

"But I did walk out and you weren't there," said Stella, much puzzled.

Philippe laughed softly.

"Ah, but I came ashore and hid in the old quarry on the hill as soon as the tide went down," he explained, "nobody seems to come up there. I shall go there again this morning until the tide is right for crossing. But first I must go to Sammy's, I should get an hour or two before anyone is about."

"Oh, Philippe, could I come too?" she pleaded.

He stood for a moment considering this.

"I don't see why not," he said, "so long as you are back in bed before anyone else gets up and starts asking questions."

"Oh, I'll be desperately careful!" she assured him, her voice rising excitedly.

"Sh!" hissed Philippe warningly, "don't go spoiling everything now, for goodness' sake."

"Sorry!" she apologised, much abashed.

"Better get a coat," he advised. "And some shoes," he added, noting her bare feet, "soft ones, though, we mustn't be heard, remember."

When they reached the outer door she whispered, "Here—better let me open it, it sometimes sticks and I sort of know the way of it."

She slid the door open without a sound and they slipped out into the silent morning. There was a chill in the air and the dune flowers were wet with dew. Stella pulled her coat closer around her and curled up her toes in the warmth of her shoes, glad that Philippe had prevented her coming barefoot. As they stepped out onto the open beach the first streaks of a golden sunrise were banding the sky in the east.

"Now, please, can you tell me what you are going to do?" pleaded Stella as they made their way across the beach towards the shore cottage.

"Well, it was my snapshots, as I told you," answered Philippe. "When I studied them again I realised we only examined one of *Evelyn Starr's* hands; we never looked into her left hand, the one that holds back the long folds of her skirt. I think we may find something in the hollow of that hand."

"What d'you think we'll find, treasure or what?" she asked.

Philippe shrugged his shoulders and spread out his hands expressively.

"I have no idea," he admitted. "But there must be something. Those two old men would not have spoken like that to Martha if there had not been some special reason. Colonel Griffiths was going to take her outside and show her something, you remember. Anyway I have got a—what is that word that Robert says?—ah yes, a 'hunch.' So! I have got a hunch that we will find something in the hollow of that second hand."

Before reaching the cottage he slowed down to warn her solemnly—

"We must be absolutely quiet, the smallest noise will disturb the animals, and they will wake Sammy."

They stole into the little yard without a sound and made straight for the figurehead. There was, as Philippe had hoped, a hollow space in the curve of the wooden hand, and he was soon kneeling on the bench probing it with eager fingers. But although he scooped out a quantity of blown sand there seemed to be nothing else in the hole. He licked a corner of his handkerchief and wiped away the dust that had accumulated in the crevices of the wood, running exploratory fingers over the surface.

"I can't feel a thing," he whispered.

Stella stood behind him, staring up at *Evelyn Starr* in frowning concentration.

"There was what he said about her jewellery, too," she murmured. "It was rather a queer thing to say, perhaps it meant something special."

"What did he say?" muttered Philippe, screwing up one eye as he tried to squint into the hollow hand with the other.

"He said her jewellery could be a help to Sammy one day. Perhaps they're real jewels. Could they be?"

Philippe straightened up to study the heavy rings and bracelets on the wooden hand and arm.

"No, they're only wood carved in one piece with the arm," he said, running a finger over them. "They'd have looked like gold when the paint was new of course, but they are only carved wood, really. Wait a minute, though!" he cried suddenly, forgetting to whisper in his excitement. "There's a screw head here, a big one, right in the middle of this large ring she's wearing. The head's been varnished over to protect it from the weather. Oh, if only we had a screwdriver!"

It was at this moment that Stella caught sight of Sammy's face pressed against the tiny bedroom window.

"Oh, dear, Sammy's seen you!" she whispered in a panic. "What now?"

Philippe swung round at once and waved a friendly hand, grinning calmly up at Sammy.

"'Morning, Sam!" he called out cheerfully, adding in an undertone to Stella, "mustn't make him suspicious whatever we do, his sort can be very obstinate at times. If he thought we didn't want him to tell he'd probably give the news to everyone. But if we don't appear to mind he may forget he's seen me at all."

"Oh, why did he have to look out now and spoil everything," moaned Stella. "Just when we were about to find the treasure."

Philippe laughed.

"Who said it's going to be treasure?" he teased. "In any case we can't do anything without a screwdriver. Can you borrow me one from the boatshed when Peter isn't there, do you think? Perhaps you could bring it to the quarry with my dinner?"

They decided it would be best if Sammy did not see them taking a special interest in the figurehead, so by the time he wandered out to join them they were tidying the woodpile. On a sudden inspiration Philippe pulled one of the pears out of his pocket and handed it to Sammy.

"A present for Willie if he likes pears," he said.

"Don't know about Willie," said Sam with his slow, sideways grin, "but I likes pears meself!" and he sank his teeth into the skin, sucking noisily at the juice. Philippe looked at his watch.

"We'll have to be going," he reminded Stella. "You must get home before you're missed."

"I'll bring up your dinner as soon as I can, and the screwdriver too," she promised as they parted at the edge of the dunes.

Stella was soon to discover that hiding a fugitive is an extremely tricky undertaking, and the morning was full of unexpected difficulties. Fortunately she was a dark-complexioned child and did not flush as easily as her fairer brothers. Nevertheless they were uncannily quick to notice that she was hiding something, particularly Robert. She no sooner started collecting her secret hoard of food than he accosted her.

"Whatever d'you want with all those pears?" he demanded. "I thought you said you were sick of them!"

"You can have one if you want it," she said quickly.

"No thanks, I'm sick of them myself. Beats me what you can want with five."

When she set off for the village it was the same. She had hoped to sneak in unnoticed with her basket, but she met Robert in the passage.

"Where have you been?" he asked.

"Only to the village," she said casually, trying to slip past him. But he barred the way, eyeing the basket with interest.

"Ah, potato crisps, good-O!" he remarked.

"They aren't for you!" she began hotly. "But do have a packet if you like," she added, changing her tactics just too late.

Robert was immediately suspicious.

"You're mighty pleasant all of a sudden," he observed. "What's up?"

"Nothing, why should there be?" said Stella lightly, skipping off to the larder. Her brother followed her with a puzzled frown.

"Something jolly well is up," he insisted. "Going off and buying grub in secret, and not even things you specially like; I've never known you choose potted shrimps before, Philippe was the only one who cared for those."

Hardest of all was the escape to the quarry. This time it was Peter who intercepted her.

"Ah, Stella, the very person I wanted," he called out as she was making her way quietly behind the shed. "Could you come in here and tie this fiddly knot for me, your fingers are neater than mine."

At any other time she would have been flattered by such a request, but now she was only conscious of poor Philippe waiting for his dinner.

When she eventually reached the quarry she found Philippe preparing to leave without even waiting for his provisions. He looked immensely relieved when he saw the basket, however.

"That looks good," he remarked, stuffing the packages into various pockets. "I thought it would have to be winkles and laverbread again! The tide is rising fast so I will have to hurry or it will be too late to cross to the island."

"Good thing it's a dull day, anyway. No one is likely to be about to see you going across," remarked Stella, glancing down at the deserted bay.

Philippe was looking longingly towards the shore cottage.

"Pity I can't go there and have another look now I've got this screwdriver," he mused. "It seems such a pity to have to waste all this good daylight."

"What about this evening when the tide goes down, surely we can try again then?" urged Stella.

"Too many people about in the evenings, I might be seen and recognised, and then someone would tell my papa and there would be telegrams and all sorts of trouble," said Philippe. "Never mind, I'll be ashore again in the morning as soon after five as I can get across. I'll go straight to Sammy's then."

"I'll meet you there with a picnic breakfast," promised Stella.

Once again their ways parted, Phillipe going cautiously down the gorse-grown hillside, keeping well under cover as he made his way towards the narrowing causeway leading to the Holm, while Stella turned back towards the village swinging her empty basket.

Chapter 9

"AH, THERE you are—been looking for you everywhere!" called Peter as Stella slipped in through the side gate on her return from the quarry the following afternoon.

"Why do you want me?" she asked cautiously, on her guard in a minute.

"Thought you might like to come and crew for me, seems a pity to waste such a grand afternoon now the storm's died down at last. It'll be high tide, too, that'll be a help when it comes to bringing the boat in again."

"Oh, Peter, how gorgeous, when? Now, at once?"

"The sooner the better as far as I'm concerned."

Stella ran round to the back of the house and pushed her empty basket in through the larder window, then hurried back to the shed.

"I can manage this lot if you can carry the rudder," said Peter, gathering up the mast, sails and oars and balancing them over his shoulder.

"Where's Robert? Isn't he coming, too?" she asked as they started out.

"Gone to Cardiff with Mum to meet his godfather, don't you remember? They'll be coming home with Dad some time late tonight."

"Oh, of course, Mummy showed me what's in the refrigerator for our supper, only I'd forgotten it was today, it all seems so long ago," said Stella, whose day had been much occupied with buying and delivering food to the hideout in the quarry.

As she followed Peter through the sand dunes she noticed that the dewberries were ripening, the low-growing bushes being covered with berries only a little less blue than the harebells nodding above them. She determined to come back later and pick some for Philippe, for although the berries were covered in blown sand this could soon be washed away, and the ripe fruit would help to ease the difficult job of collecting enough provisions for the ever-hungry stowaway in the quarry. Her thoughts turned to him now, and she sighed as she remembered the disappointments of the morning. For nothing had gone according to plan. To begin with the tide had kept him a prisoner on Long Holm a good half hour later than expected, and then when they met at the shore cottage they found Sammy already out and about. This was a cruel blow, for the harder they tried to turn his interest elsewhere, the more closely he watched their movements, making it quite impossible to work on the figurehead as planned. Consequently, Philippe had gone up to the quarry in a mood of black despair, which had not entirely disappeared when she took up his dinner.

When they reached the final gap in the dunes her eyes turned at once to the Holm and she saw that it was already cut off, the causeway just awash with the rising tide. She pictured Philippe sitting out there in her cave, and hoped he was working out some plan to simplify things when they met at Sammy's the following morning.

There were still a good many people about on the beach, chiefly visitors from the caravan site, making the most of the improvement in the weather. There were a number of people bathing, too, and a chattering party of small boys undressing under the big dune near which the *Evening Star* was lying. Stella watched the group for a moment, amused by a particularly skinny little fellow who was a good deal more interested in the *Evening Star* than in the rubber dinghy he was inflating. As he paused to stare openmouthed at the boat, Stella could imagine how enviously he must be comparing her with his own inferior craft. However, his musings were brought to an abrupt end when an older boy shouted roughly—

"Get on with yer blowing, Bill, we're nearly ready."

Peter's voice broke in on her own musings no less peremptorily: "Come on, Stella, for goodness' sake, and give a hand instead of mooning there."

She swung round guiltily to find him already up-ending the mast, preparatory to stepping it.

"Keep those halyards out of the way, will you," he called.

She pulled the trailing ropes aside as he slid the mast into position.

For the next ten minutes or so she was kept so busy that she forgot the boys until she became aware of a silent group behind her, watching every detail of the preparations with breathless interest. When everything was ready, they fell into place without a word and helped to haul the boat down to the edge of the sea on the trolley. They helped slide her into the water, and when Peter turned back to attend to the trolley he discovered that one of the boys had already pulled it back to its place under the sand dunes. The rest of the group stood ankle deep in the water, silently watching Peter's final arrangements. Stella knew just how determined he must be to make a really professional start in front of such an audience.

Fortunately, the wind was off the shore and the waves small enough to make the start an easy one, and they were soon draw-

ing away from the beach as smoothly as even Peter could wish. When Stella had time to look back the boys had returned for their own rubber dinghy which they were carrying down to the sea between them, the sound of their voices reaching her fitfully on the off-shore wind.

But there were more engrossing things to attend to than children on the beach, and soon all her attention was centred on the curve of the wind-filled sail and the thrilling sound of the water rippling under their bow as the little boat raced across the bay.

"Wind's absolutely perfect," said Peter with satisfaction. "While it's blowing steadily from this quarter we can make good long reaches parallel with the shore, which is much better than heading out to sea, with the Race looking as angry as it does today."

At his words Stella turned her eyes to the ugly tumble of rough water running obliquely off the end of Long Holm, and she shivered, knowing very well how dangerous this particular current could be at certain states of the tide.

"The Race seems a good name for it today," she remarked, her gaze held fascinated by the long procession of white-capped waves that never appeared to break.

After a couple of reaches across the bay, Peter said casually, "Like to take her yourself for a bit?"

"Oh, Pete, could I really?" she gasped, suddenly cold all over with excitement. She had known she would learn to sail one day, of course, but somehow she hadn't expected the chance to come so soon.

She waited for Peter to give the order and then crawled aft to change places, both of them moving very carefully so as not to upset the balance of the boat. Then she found herself gripping the tiller in one hand and the mainsheet in the other. Peter leant towards her, telling her what to do.

"Let her out a little . . . that's right . . . just a little more, you'll soon feel when she catches the wind—ah, there you are!" As he spoke the boat leapt forward and the lovely rippling sound could be heard again under her bow.

"That's fine," he remarked approvingly, but five minutes later, just as she was beginning to relax and almost enjoy herself, he announced that it was time to go about and her anxieties started all over again.

"Bring her up into the wind," he directed. "That's it, don't be afraid of it. Now round you go—mind your head as the boom comes over."

Stella gripped the tiller and clenched her teeth as she followed his instructions. For a moment everything was quiet; then, just as she wondered if she had done something wrong, the wind caught the flapping sail on the other side, the boom swung over sharply, and as the sail filled once more the boat sprang forward like a living creature suddenly set free.

"Well done!" smiled Peter. "I can see you are going to make a really useful member of the crew."

Stella beamed, too happy to speak. She knew she had been a failure over the building of the boat, but now she began to realise that handling it was quite another matter, and she determined that she would learn to sail it just as competently as her brothers.

As her confidence grew, she relaxed enough to experiment a little and was thrilled to discover how promptly the boat responded to the lightest touch on the tiller. They were running in towards the headland, and Stella's attention was divided between the business of keeping the sail full of wind and steering a straight course. Peter, however, had time to look about him, and presently his eyes turned to Long Holm. Although a considerable channel of water was already running between the rocks and the shore, the island itself was not yet divided, the three hummocks being still joined to one another by low-lying rocks.

Stella was expecting the order to go about, but Peter had a totally different plan in mind.

"How about landing on Long Holm," he suggested. "The sea is high enough, and calm enough, too, to allow us to come right into the cowrie bay."

Stella's heart skipped a beat and although she opened her mouth to make some feeble objection, no sound came out. Perhaps this was really just as well, for what could she say that would not make Peter suspicious? They had so often talked about this project during the building of the boat, and she had been keener than anyone to land on Long Holm when it was an island. But she had not guessed that when the time came, Philippe would be out there as a fugitive, with herself the only person in all the world who knew where he was hiding.

It was unlikely, she knew, that Peter would visit the cave or her part of the island. But there was always the danger that Philippe, believing himself alone on the Holm, might come out of hiding to collect shellfish or driftwood for the fire, feeling quite safe from observation as long as he kept to the seaward side of the island. And it was, of course, this seaward side that they were now approaching.

Fortunately, Peter was too concerned with the details of navigation to notice her lack of enthusiasm.

"Better let me take her now," he advised. "Then you can get into the bow and keep a lookout for rocks as we go in."

After changing places he brought the boat head to wind and they lowered the sails.

"We'll take her in under oars," he explained. "Then you can

fend off with the boat-hook if necessary. We must raise the centreboard, too; we want to draw as little water as possible while we are in among the rocks."

Stella attended to the centreboard while Peter stowed the sails where they would not be in the way of the oars.

"I'll make straight for Robert's island," he explained. "There should be plenty of depth in the cowrie bay at this state of the tide. I'll edge her in as gently as I can. Be ready with the boat-hook, and sing out if you see any rocks under water."

Stella found it hard to look for underwater rocks while she was anxiously scanning the island, fearing to see a dark head bob up on the skyline! However she saw no sign of a movement on shore, so was able to give most of her attention to the job in hand, and they slid in between the rocks without mishap. The tiny bay enclosed the *Evening Star* as though designed to be her private harbour.

They jumped ashore and between them pulled her up the shingle.

"She'll be O.K. there," said Peter. "Here's this morning's tide line well below where she's lying now."

"How long before high water?" questioned Stella, eyeing the low-lying rocks that lay between Robert's island and her own.

Peter looked at his watch.

"About three quarters of an hour—just time for me to see if I can find any trace of an oystercatcher's nest—not that there ever is much trace, of course. But I'm pretty sure they must have nested somewhere on my island."

Stella waited until Peter reached his island before turning towards her own. Then she hurried across the dividing rocks, jumping over the intervening gullies until she reached the final sharp upthrust of rock. At the top of this she turned to wave to Peter.

But he was already doubled up among his own rocks, too absorbed in his search to think about anything else.

She turned in the direction of the cave and at once became aware of a curious smell. A moment later she saw the sight she had been dreading to see since the moment of landing on the Holm—a twist of smoke drifting up from the vicinity of the cave.

She sprang forward and saw Philippe crouched on the ledge below her. He was carefully feeding small sticks into a bright little fire on which bubbled a steaming can. He looked up startled as she slithered down on to the ledge beside him.

"Quick! You must put out that fire before Peter sees the smoke," she panted incoherently.

A rebellious scowl crossed the boy's face, but his voice was calm as he replied, "There is no smoke, not enough to be seen from the shore anyway. I'm keeping the flames bright on purpose, so that it doesn't smoke, you see. But I must keep the fire going until my winkles are cooked. How did you get here, by the way?"

"There is smoke. I saw it myself before I even saw the fire. Honestly, Philippe, we'll simply have to put it out at once if you don't want to be discovered."

Philippe glanced up and saw that she was serious. With a small impatient sigh he reached for a strip of driftwood. With this he managed to scoop a steaming winkle out of the can.

"It seems to be cooked all right," he remarked, examining it critically. Then removing the can from the flames, he added, "O.K. then, you can do what you like with the fire now, I've finished with it anyway."

Without further hesitation Stella seized a long stick from the pile of driftwood and plunging it into the heart of the fire shovelled out the burning sticks and sent them hurtling down into the gully below.

"There won't be much smoke from those anyway!" she remarked, looking down on the scattered fragments with satisfaction.

"But how did you get here? That's what I want to know," said Philippe, squatting back on his heels and smiling expectantly. "Like to try a winkle while you tell me?"

But Stella was not smiling.

"Look, Philippe, this is serious, really it is. Peter is here on the island with us and he's quite likely to discover you any minute if you don't watch out!"

That soon took the smile off Philippe's face, and he was as sober as she could wish as she went on—

"We came out for a sail in the *Evening Star*, and suddenly Peter suggested landing on Long Holm like we've always wanted to do. I couldn't see how to put him off without making him suspicious."

Philippe nodded understandingly.

"I see what you mean," he said. "Where is he now?"

"Gone over to his own island to see if the oystercatchers nested there. But actually, Philippe, I've been wondering would it really matter if Pete did see you? I mean, it isn't as though he's a grownup, he wouldn't send you back to Brittany."

To her surprise a wary look crept into the French boy's eyes.

"You can't be sure," he muttered. "When people get as old as Peter they have queer ideas sometimes. After all, he's nearly grown up and a prefect at school and everything. He might easily think my parents would be worrying."

"But why should they worry?" she objected. "They think

you're in Roscoff with your uncle. He might worry though, I suppose."

"He doesn't know I was coming. You see I forgot to mail the letter my mother wrote to him. I found it in my pocket when I got to Roscoff. By then it was too late to explain, my uncle was getting ready to sail and was much too busy to be bothered with me. So Yves said it would be best for me to stow away—and more fun, too, of course! Anyway I'll be all right here, now this fire is out. I'll hide in the cave and not come out until the tide has ebbed a bit. I'll be safe then, because you will have to get the *Evening Star* away long before low water. But," he added with his sudden grin, "I must just go to the top and see what Peter's doing now!"

"Oh, no! That's silly, he might easily turn round and see you," she protested. "I'll go up and look myself, and come back and report to you if you like."

But Philippe could never resist this sort of risk and was already crawling up the rocks towards the crest of the island. There was nothing for Stella to do but join him, and they were soon lying side by side on an uncomfortable ridge of jagged rocks sparsely cushioned with samphire. The smell of the crushed plants surrounded them as they rested their chins on the rock, peering through the brittle stems of long-dried sea-pinks.

Below where they lay the narrowing line of rocks still stretched across to Robert's island where the tall mast of the *Evening Star* rose from the cowrie bay. Peter's island lay beyond, and they could just make out the green hump of his jersey where he crouched among the rocks.

"He'll not see me!" laughed Philippe.

At this moment a sudden piercing scream rang out across the Holm, and turning in the direction of the sound they saw a

rubber dinghy drifting rapidly past the cowrie bay towards the open sea. Something could just be seen waving above the inflated rim.

"Oh, it must be those boys we saw!" gasped Stella in horror.

Philippe did not waste time on words. He sprang to his feet and went leaping across the rocks towards the bay where the *Evening Star* was lying. It was all Stella could do to keep pace with him.

"Call Peter," he commanded as he seized the boat and started

dragging her into the water. But although they called with all the strength of their lungs, their shouts were carried away on the off-shore wind in the wake of the drifting dinghy.

"I'll have to go and fetch him, he'll never hear," panted Stella, starting to scramble over the rocks.

"No, no, we haven't time, I need your help here," called Philippe. "Get into the bow and keep a lookout for rocks while I get her clear."

The boat shot out into deep water as he spoke, and in a surprisingly short time he had rowed her clear of the rocks into the comparative safety of the deep water beyond.

"We must get up the sails at once," he said briefly, as with sure hands he caught hold of the halyards, and with no more than a couple of swift commands to Stella had the sails hoisted.

"Lower the centreboard now," he called out, taking it for granted that she could manage, while he leant across to take the tiller as the boat got under way. The centreboard was heavy, but she succeeded in lowering it without delay. Once this was done, and the rowlocks safely stowed away, she had time to spare for the object of their trip.

Chapter 10

PEERING under the foresail Stella saw that the rubber dinghy was being swept along at an alarming rate and was already well out to sea. She could see no sign of a passenger, nor could they hear any cries for help, since the wind was now behind them.

"It's getting stronger, that's the trouble," muttered Philippe. However, his long familiarity with boats enabled him to make the most of the freshening wind, and before very long it was evident that they were gaining on the dinghy.

They were also drawing steadily closer to the Race. Stella shivered as she looked at the tumbled breakers, hearing already the rustle of the agitated water. But although her fingers tightened their grip on the centreboard case she said nothing, knowing that if the dinghy and its passenger should be swept into the Race they would have to follow.

As soon as they were near enough to have some hope of being heard by anyone aboard the dinghy they yelled in unison—

"Hi! Ahoy! Are you there? We're coming to save you!"

Looking anxiously under the sail Stella caught a glimpse of a small white face raised for a moment above the rounded rim of the dinghy.

"We're coming!" she shouted again. "We're catching up with you."

It was some time, however, before they did catch up, and an even longer time before they were able to get a grip on the slippery rubber surface and fasten a rope to one of the lifelines.

Stella now saw that its occupant was Bill, the skinny small boy she had noticed on the beach. But now he was shuddering with cold and terror, and quite incapable of catching the end of a rope when it was thrown to him. As a result, Philippe had to manoeuvre the boat into a position from which Stella was able to reach across herself and fasten the rope to a lifeline with one of the knots she had recently learnt.

"Now work her round astern if you can," ordered Philippe. "Then I'll tie her to the *Evening Star*. Keep a firm hold of your end of the line, whatever you do."

To make things still more difficult Bill suddenly dragged himself to his knees, and, leaning perilously over the rim of the dinghy, screamed to be taken on board.

"*Tiens! Tiens!* Wait a minute!" shouted Philippe. "We must make fast first before you get swept out of reach again."

Not understanding a word that was said the child burst into loud hiccoughing sobs, which were only silenced when a wave splashed up between the boats with unexpected suddenness, soaking him to the skin.

The job of transferring Bill from the tossing dinghy into the *Evening Star* proved to be the hardest part of the whole operation. Stella wondered if she ever could have kept her grip on the child if she hadn't already had the experience of rescuing the sheep on launching day.

Only when Bill was safely aboard did she notice the waves tumbling all about them, seeming to come from several directions at once.

"Why, it's suddenly got quite rough!" she observed in surprise. Then, glancing ahead she saw smooth water beyond the waves and realised what had happened.

"Oh, Philippe, we've got into the Race, haven't we?" she said in a small high voice quite unlike her own.

Philippe nodded briefly. He had enough to tackle without bothering with conversation. Bill, on the other hand, was beginning to perk up, and although his teeth still chattered he managed to smile as he remarked, "I always wanted to sail in this 'ere boat when I seed 'er on the bay. I don't like that old dinghy, not now I don't."

Stella pulled off her jersey and draped it round the shivering little boy. To her relief his conversation stopped as abruptly as it had started, and he sagged against her, suddenly fast asleep, worn out with fright and cold. She slipped an arm around him and held him close, as much for her own comfort as his.

The tumbling waves seemed bigger than ever now, slopping over the sides of the boat from time to time to swish to and fro under the bottom boards. A handkerchief, dropped from the sleeve of her jersey, was blown overboard, and before it had time to sink it was carried away on the crest of a wave, accentuating the terrifying speed of the current.

"I don't know if it's best to lower the sails or keep on as we are. I've never sailed in anything like this before," confessed Philippe, speaking to himself rather than Stella. She remained silent; there seemed to be nothing to say. Presently Philippe spoke again.

"We have not shipped very much water, have we?" he asked.

"Oh, no, not much, it sounds worse than it is," said Stella, leaning down to peer between the slats under her feet.

"Think I'll keep on like this for the present then," he decided. "We ought to pull out of it soon if the wind doesn't drop; we have only such a small way to go, not more than a few metres now between ourselves and the safe water—you'd think we'd have pulled out long ago."

The wind held, but in spite of this it took a considerable time to cross those last few yards of tumbled water into the calm beyond. Then, quite suddenly it was over—for a moment the *Evening Star* appeared to hesitate, as though testing the reality of the smooth water under her keel. Then her sails filled and she leapt forward eagerly, sailing freely again at last. As Stella let out a long sigh of relief she wondered how long she had really been holding her breath.

"Phew!" said Philippe. It was little enough to say, but he said it in such a way that it sounded quite a lot.

Although the *Evening Star* was clear of the Race, she was a tremendous distance from the shore, and they were faced with a long slow beat against the strong head wind. Added to which, the sun was already low in the sky, so it looked as though it might well be dark before they landed.

"How's the kid?" asked Philippe suddenly, becoming really aware of their passenger for the first time.

"Asleep," said Stella. "And he's stopped shivering at last, thank goodness." She had only just stopped shivering herself, but she did not mention this.

"She's a grand little boat, she can sail so close to the wind," remarked Philippe, nodding towards the curving sail. "And that is a help when we have a wind so strong against us. I hope it won't fall light though, it so often does when the sun goes down."

Stella turned to look at the sky where clouds were already massing in the west, preparing for a spectacular sunset. They sailed on in silence, Philippe sailing as close to the wind as possible while they beat back and forth across the bay, each tack bringing them closer to the shore.

The sunset was short-lived and clouds obscured the sun even before it dipped behind the headland. For a while light lingered

in the sky as it dimmed from green to lavender, and the last of the colour drained from the sea around them.

"Oh, look!" cried Stella suddenly. "There's the evening star, the real one. That's the second time we've seen it from the boat." And then as full realisation dawned on her she added in an awestruck tone, "And do you realise? This is the second time our own *Evening Star* has saved a life!"

The first lights soon began to twinkle in the village and Stella scanned the skyline, trying to pick out her own home in the deepening dusk. But there seemed to be no light anywhere near where the house should be, and she was puzzled until she remembered that her parents were in Cardiff and would not be home till late. Then, for the first time since leaving Long Holm, she remembered Peter.

"Philippe!" she cried, aghast, "I've only just remembered Peter out there on the Holm all this time!" She turned her eyes in the direction of the island, but although the black mass of the headland stood out distinctly against the sky, the rocks at its base could no longer be distinguished against the darkened water. Nor was it possible to see whether the causeway was uncovered. And, since it was now too dark to see their watches, they had no idea of the state of the tide.

"Well, we'll soon be in now, anyway," said Philippe. "I can hear the waves on the beach at last, although I can't quite see them yet."

By the time they eventually drew in to the beach the last of the picnic parties had long gone home. Nevertheless, a line of figures could be discerned strung out along the water's edge, and long before the boat was in reach they plunged out to meet her, up to their waists in water, and a dozen scared boys' voices called in chorus—

"Did you get 'im? Bill, say Bill, are you O.K.? Hi! Billy, are you there?"

"He's O.K.," Philippe assured them, while Stella roused the sleepy little boy at her side so that they could all see for themselves that he was alive and well.

Then another figure splashed out from the shore calling "Stella! Stella! Are you there?" and Peter thrust his way through the crowd and laid his hands on the boat. As Stella called out reassuringly he leant closer to discover who was at the helm, and burst out in amazed disbelief—

"*Philippe!* . . . how on earth . . . ?"

"Let's get the boat in first and talk afterwards," suggested Philippe, realising for the first time how completely exhausted he was.

With so many hands to help them the boat was soon beached. Then, while two of the boys ran to fetch the trolley, the rest proceeded to hustle poor Billy into his clothes, impressing on him meanwhile that the adventure must not be mentioned to anyone at home, anyway not until his mum was safely out of hospital, since she would be sure to get in a "state." One of them unfastened and deflated the rubber dinghy, while several others hoisted the *Evening Star* onto her trolley and pulled her back to her place below the sand dunes. Philippe and Peter followed with the sails and oars. When they reached the boat they discovered that their helpers had melted off into the darkness.

"Oh, well, they've had enough of a scare for one day, poor kids," said Peter, remembering the terrified group he had joined at the edge of the sea.

They stood propped against the boat for a while, Philippe and Stella telling the story of the last few days, while Peter described his own feelings on discovering that both the boat and

Stella had vanished from Long Holm. He had never spotted the rubber dinghy, but he had seen the *Evening Star* running steadily out to sea.

"I thought at first she was drifting," he said. "Then I realised that her sails were up and knew that somebody must be sailing her. I was scared I can tell you, specially when I saw her getting into the Race."

"I suppose you thought it must be me sailing her?" said Stella hopefully.

"I just didn't know what to think," he admitted. "I hunted all over the Holm for you, and by the time the tide was low enough for me to pick my way over the causeway it was nearly dark. Then I found those kids on the beach and heard about the drifting dinghy which gave me the probable reason for the *Evening Star*'s dash out to sea. The boys insisted they had seen you overtake the dinghy although they had lost sight of it after that. But I still couldn't see how you could possibly be sailing the boat on your own like that, after only one lesson. By Jove, Philippe, it's a good thing you were here, else that kid would have been lost for sure. I never could have caught up with him myself, I don't know enough about sailing yet."

"I couldn't have done it myself without Stella's help," declared Philippe. "She was the one who grabbed the dinghy and hung onto it, too, when we got into the Race."

"Lucky you saw it drifting out," said Peter. "Those kids were far too scared to go for help. I guess they aren't really allowed to use that dinghy on their own at all. It seems that everyone else had left the beach by the time it drifted out. And of course a strong off-shore wind like this is the most dangerous thing of all, it would blow him out of his depth in no time."

"Yes, he was travelling pretty fast," agreed Philippe reflectively.

"You know," said Stella in a thoughtful tone, "it isn't only those boys who mustn't say a word about all this, it's us, too. You see nobody must know that Philippe is here at all—he's supposed to be in Roscoff with his uncle."

"Well, one thing is definite," said Peter very decidedly, "wherever you're supposed to be, you aren't spending the night in that cave, not after the experience you've had this afternoon. You can come in with me tonight, the others won't be in till late, and we can smuggle you out in the morning early and nobody the wiser!"

As a result of this arrangement the trio sat down to a very cheerful supper in the kitchen, and Philippe went over the details of his stowaway trip again for their entertainment.

They washed up carefully after the meal, clearing everything away so that there was nothing to show that three had eaten instead of the expected two.

"All the same," remarked Philippe, eyeing what was left of the jelly, "your mother will think you two were awfully hungry."

"We often are," observed Peter.

"Anyway," said Stella, "I bet it was a nicer meal than half-warmed winkles, wasn't it?"

Chapter 11

NOW THAT Peter was included in the secret, Stella's trips to the quarry became a good deal easier, for she now had an ally to cover her tracks in place of a second suspicious watcher questioning every movement. He suggested, just as Philippe had feared he would, that the Griveaus ought to be told of their son's whereabouts, and he was only partially satisfied when the other two pointed out that in any case, Philippe would now be back in Brittany almost as soon as a letter could reach his parents.

"It seems a pity to worry them if we needn't," murmured Philippe.

Peter did not believe for one moment that they would really find any solution to Sammy's problem hidden in the old figurehead. However this did not stop him from being extremely helpful in hiding Philippe and organising his getaway next morning. And it was Peter who had a brilliant inspiration at the secret six o'clock breakfast in the boatshed.

"But why on earth should you wait till dusk to start on the job?" he said. "Why not disguise yourself, then you could work in the daylight. If you put on a sports coat and sunglasses and some sort of a hat no one will guess you aren't just one of the ordinary summer visitors, specially if you aren't seen going down through the village with Stella. I'll see what I can find upstairs and Stella can bring the things along with your provisions."

When Stella arrived in the quarry with an armful of clothes, Philippe was delighted.

"Do I look like an English visitor?" he asked, getting into the sports coat right away.

It was a trifle wide in the shoulders, but no one was likely to notice a detail like that. By the time he had put on the hat and glasses he looked such a totally different person that Stella doubled up with laughter.

"You look just like a tripper on a mystery tour!" she giggled. "Let's go down to the cottage now. You can go by the back lane, nobody's likely to see you there, and if they do they'll never guess who you really are, you look so different. As to Sammy, he'll not worry one way or the other, he's much too worried over Henry."

"Henry?" questioned Philippe.

"Yes, that's his slow worm, you remember. It's disappeared again, and poor Sammy's still hopefully looking for it. Now, shall we go? There's your lane. I'll meet you in the sand dunes."

As they reached the shore a woman turned into the dunes beyond them. "That was Mrs. Jenkins," reported Stella. "She and three others take turns going down to see to Sammy's dinner every day. He gets breakfast and tea himself, and he could manage dinner, too, of course, but they like to look in and make sure he's all right—everyone's fond of Sammy."

"Yes, the neighbours are generally good to the children of God," said Philippe.

They found Sammy crouched at the foot of the wall, poking his fingers into a crevice.

"Henry's gone again," he told them dolefully, scarcely troubling to glance in their direction. This made it easy for Philippe to concentrate on the figurehead. Pulling the screwdriver out of his pocket, he knelt on the bench and got to work on the screw head right away. It proved to be unexpectedly stiff after being embedded in varnish for so long. Stella held her breath as she watched.

"I have to be careful not to break it," muttered Philippe between clenched teeth. Suddenly Stella saw him relax and knew that he must have felt the screw begin to move. Soon he was able to turn it freely and he gave a small grunt of satisfaction as he finally pulled it out. It was a large screw, considerably longer than he had expected. He measured it against the outer curve of *Evelyn Starr*'s hand.

"It was put in at a funny angle," he mused, "right through the palm of her hand—the end of it must be just about here, in the fold of her dress." He ran his fingers over the fold in question. Suddenly he stiffened.

"What is it?" whispered Stella, pressing closer.

Philippe made no attempt to answer. Instead he felt in his pocket for a penknife, and opening the smaller blade he began to scrape away the flaking paint from the portion of the fold held back by the curving fingers. Working very gently he soon laid bare enough wood to show that there was indeed a join. Further scraping revealed a second join some four inches higher up.

"You see!" he exulted, his eyes alight in a face grown pale with excitement. "A small piece of wood has been inserted into her skirt just here. I must pull it out, it should slip out quite easily."

It did not slip out quite easily, however.

"Something seems to be holding it back," he muttered.

"Perhaps there's another screw," suggested Stella, getting onto the bench and bending over the wooden hand. "Yes, look, surely this is one?" and she pointed to the gilded centre of one of the ornate medallions adorning the clumsy bracelet.

Philippe was up on the bench beside her in an instant.

"Here, let me get at it," he said, edging past her with the screwdriver. "This one's been driven in at a different angle, it must enter the fold somewhere about here, several centimetres from the other one," and he tapped the carved fold behind the wooden fingers.

"The hollow of her hand," mused Stella softly. "So you were right after all."

Philippe soon loosened the screw. After this he was able to pull out the section of the fold it had been holding in place. It proved to be a wooden board measuring approximately twelve inches by six. Since the panel itself was scarcely more than an inch in thickness the opening it left in the flowing skirt was too narrow to allow Philippe to insert his hand beyond the knuckles.

"I can't even feel to the back, and it's too dark to see into the space at all," he complained, screwing up his eyes in an attempt to see beyond the narrow opening.

Stella's own eyes fell on the board in his hand. On one of the shorter edges, two small holes pierced the wood, showing where the screws had entered the panel, holding it in position. Beyond this point the smooth surface was covered with what appeared to be lettering, lightly scored into the smooth wood as though someone had written the words with a pointed tool.

"Look, Philippe, perhaps the board itself is what we are looking for, there seems to be writing on it," she ventured.

Philippe spun round.

"It's lettering all right," he agreed as they bent over the board together. But the damp of years had discoloured it, and although they could feel the letters with their finger tips they could not see them clearly.

"I know what we might do," began Stella. "Only would it work, I wonder?"

"Would what work?" demanded Philippe eagerly.

"Well, when we were little we used to make what we called ghost pictures. There was a gold elephant's head on the cover of the Jungle Books, and we used to put tracing paper over it, and then blacken the paper all over with pencil until we had a ghost picture of the elephant—it was clearer than the one on the book, I remember. Do you think we might make a ghost copy of this writing and see if it is clear enough to read? We could use the paper bag I brought those biscuits in. The only thing is, have you got a pencil?"

Luckily, Philippe had a pencil, and he sharpened it carefully while Stella emptied the paper bag and shook out all the crumbs. Then Philippe laid the board on the bench, slit the paper bag in two, and spread the less crumpled half over the lettering on the board, smoothing it out as flat as possible before getting to work with the pencil.

"You want to do it with the side of the pencil point," directed Stella, leaning over his shoulder. Soon white letters began to appear as he darkened the area surrounding them.

"Oh, it's coming up beautifully!" she breathed. "We'll surely be able to read it in a minute."

"There!" smiled Philippe when the job was complete. "Now let us see what it says."

But as he removed the hand with which he had been holding the sheet in place, a sudden gust of wind swirled around the yard, sweeping the precious paper over the wall.

Stella was after it in an instant, almost falling over Sammy who was still grovelling under the wall in search of Henry.

Beyond the shelter of the cottage the wind was blowing steadily, and the flimsy sheet of paper was already well on its way to the sea, skidding and dancing over the smooth sand. Every time she stooped to pick it up, it whirled out of reach again. As a result she was breathless and panting by the time she finally captured it on the very edge of the tide. She snatched it up, and without waiting to read it, sped back over the sand to the shore cottage. She burst into the yard to find Philippe just completing a second ghost rubbing.

"I've made a new copy on the other half of the paper bag," he told her, and holding the page firmly in place with his thumb he called her across to read it with him. It was at this moment that a step sounded on the stones behind them and a voice demanded sharply—

"And what do you think you are doing?"

Stella spun round to find Mr. Griffiths behind her.

"So it's you again!" he said frowning. "Didn't you see the notice on the gate? Surely you know this place is up for sale? Very well then, since the property is already in the agents' hands I should prefer you not to meddle with anything here before the sale, since I mean to get a good price for this cottage if I can."

Stella shuffled her feet uncomfortably. But when she glanced out of the sides of her eyes, she saw that Philippe was standing in a trance, reading the paper in his hand with an expression on his face that she could not understand. When he finally spoke. She found it hard to believe what she heard.

"But I am not sure that it truly is your cottage, sir," he answered very quietly.

His face was so grave and his tone so obviously sincere that

Mr. Griffiths could see, as she could, that the boy had no thought of being rude.

"You can see it all here for yourself, sir," he explained, holding out the board with its ghost transcription. "Old Captain Walters told Martha that *Evelyn Starr* carried Sammy's security in the hollow of her hand. This must be what he meant."

Mr. Griffiths wasn't listening. He had turned from the board to the paper copy, and was staring at this with a face that had become a good deal paler than Philippe's. After studying the signatures that completed the page he mumbled in a bewildered manner, "Yes, that's my father's signature all right—William George Griffiths, and that's Captain Walters' underneath, cut into the softness of the wood with something hard, a carpenter's pencil, I daresay, he always had such things about him."

Stella stood looking from one face to the other, wondering what in the world it was all about. There was a strange expression on Mr. Griffiths' face, something that made her thankful when Philippe took her by the arm and propelled her gently out of the gate.

Leaving the cottage they turned towards the village, Philippe walking so rapidly that Stella had to run to keep pace with him.

"Now, Philippe, please explain, does it tell where to find the treasure or what?" she panted. "And, anyway, need we go so fast?"

Philippe strode on in silence, and glancing at his face she decided not to ask him any more. Only once, halfway up the deserted village street, did he pause for a moment, turning to where she was hurrying along behind him.

"To tell the truth I almost wish we'd never discovered this at all," he said grimly, "except, I suppose, for Sammy's sake. Poor Mr. Griffiths, though . . . it's hard for him . . ."

Stella was more confused than ever, but there was something about Philippe in this mood that made it impossible to question him. She did, however, find her voice when they reached her home and he threw open the gate and started towards the house.

"Not in there!" she gasped. "You're forgetting! If you go that way they'll see you!"

She might as well have spoken to the gatepost; Philippe strode on, completely unconcerned, and, seeing the french windows open, walked straight into the house.

Mr. Bevan had just got home from work, and his wife was bringing in the tea tray as Philippe stepped into the room. There was a moment's astonished silence during which Mrs. Bevan hastily dumped the tray on the nearest chair.

"Philippe!" she gasped, "where on earth have you sprung from?"

"I had to come back to find this," he explained, taking the crumpled paper from Stella, "and now I think I wish we hadn't found it."

"What is it, anyway?" asked Mr. Bevan, holding out his hand for the paper. His wife hurried across to read it over his shoulder, and Stella leant on the arm of his chair, reading too.

It was an astonishing document, made all the odder by the fact that Philippe had had to use a paper bag covered in blue and green advertisements, which blended strangely with the spidery white lettering running across the pencil-blackened page. But, however odd the general effect, the meaning of the words was plain enough, as were the signatures at the foot of the paper.

"What an extraordinary business," muttered Mr. Bevan. "Where did you get this anyway?" he asked, turning to Philippe. Stella could scarcely curb her impatience while Phillippe decribed how they had found the panel and rubbed the message from it with a pencil and a paper bag. As soon as he paused for breath she burst out—

"Yes, but what does it mean exactly?"

Before there was a chance for anyone to answer the door opened and Peter and Robert came in. Robert stopped dead in his tracks. "What on earth . . . ?" he began. But nobody even noticed him. Philippe was staring questioningly at Mr. Bevan, and so were Stella and her mother.

"Does it mean," began Stella slowly, "that Sammy and Mr. Griffiths were swapped when they were babies, and that Mr. Griffiths isn't really Mr. Griffiths at all, and Sammy isn't really Sammy?"

"Why, yes, I suppose that is about the gist of it," replied her father thoughtfully.

The boys in the doorway strode across the room, leaning over to read the paper in their turn.

"But what could have been the point of it, and why the secrecy?" puzzled Mrs. Bevan.

"Why, surely that part's clear enough," said her husband. "It obviously goes back to the early days when the two men lost their wives in the influenza epidemic."

"Ah, yes," interrupted his wife, "and Colonel Griffiths' baby caught it too, you remember. And," she went on more slowly, "that baby has become the Sammy that we know today, of course. So perhaps he never quite recovered after all, and that it was that early illness that left him a little simple."

Mr. Bevan nodded thoughtfully.

"Yes indeed, that is a likely explanation," he agreed. "Anyhow, whatever the cause, it must soon have been clear to the Colonel that his son would never be fit to carry on the running of the estate after his own day."

"Poor man," murmured Mrs. Bevan, "it must have been a terrible blow to him, he always looked on the estate as a sacred trust; and rightly, too, since most of the villagers depended on him for their livelihood as well as their homes."

"That's evidently what he's referring to here," said her husband, tapping the paper as he spoke. "He mentions the fact that the whole village would be affected, and many people faced with actual hardship, if there was no one to carry on his duties after his death."

"But hadn't he any other relations who could have looked after the place if his son wasn't fit to do it?" demanded Peter.

"Ah, that would have been the trouble, of course," said Mrs. Bevan. "The Colonel's only brother was a complete waster, and he was known to have asserted more than once that if he were ever to have control of the estate he would sell the lot to the highest bidder immediately, with absolutely no consideration for the unfortunate villagers. The Colonel was too good a man to risk such a disaster to his much-loved tenants. But what a terrible problem it must have been for him."

"But why did he choose the Captain's son, I wonder?" mused Philippe, speaking for the first time.

"Well, Captain Walters was his trusted friend, remember," said Mr. Bevan, "the two had known one another all their lives. So, since his friend also had a son, a fine, healthy child but motherless, and homeless too, at this time as it happened, it probably occurred to him that if the child of such a father were to be taken in hand young enough, he could be trained to run the estate as it should be run, for the good of the whole community."

"But if Captain Walters was such a nice man, then how could he bear to give away his own little baby and bring up another one instead?" demanded Stella fiercely.

It was her mother who replied, "Don't you think he might have seen it as a wonderful opportunity for his little boy?" she suggested. "It was a chance in life such as he himself could never hope to give him."

"Besides, it wasn't as though either man would lose sight of his own child after the changeover," continued Mr. Bevan. "The Captain spent most of his time at sea in any case, and he would now see his boy grow up in circumstances far better than anything he could offer. As for Colonel Griffiths, he could visit the shore cottage whenever he pleased, and he must have realised what a particularly happy home it would be for a handicapped child. No one could have been kinder than Martha."

"I suppose even she didn't know who Sammy really was?" mused Mrs. Bevan.

"Evidently not. I suppose the fewer who knew the better in the circumstances. However, they clearly planned to tell her the truth once their arrangements were complete."

"Why would it matter if people knew?" asked Robert.

"Well, obviously the Colonel's brother would have been the first to contest such an unorthodox arrangement. Also, I dare say the villagers might have resented being overlorded by the son of a simple man like Captain Walters, however much they respected him as a person."

"You'd think somebody'd have been bound to suspect and let it out," said Peter. "What about the servants who looked after the Colonel's baby before they were changed? And Captain Walters' old mother who had charge of the real little Sammy?"

"No one but two old servants saw the Colonel's baby in the months following the epidemic; although there must have been a doctor of course, your father, I presume?" said Mr. Bevan turning suddenly to his wife.

She nodded, laughing reminiscently.

"I never knew anyone better at guarding people's secrets than my father," she remarked. "He certainly never hinted to us that anything unusual was going on, although he must undoubtedly have known, since he nursed both families through the epidemic. As for the Manor servants, only two were left, remember, and they were pensioned off before the changeover took place."

"And what about Captain Walters' mother?" persisted Peter.

"She lived far away in Wiltshire, don't forget, and in those days people didn't get about the country as they do today. But in any case, they were simple people, quite likely the old woman couldn't even read or write, and would have no means of keeping in touch once her son took the baby back to Wales. And now I come to think of it, I'm pretty sure she died soon after his return, in any case."

"What about Martha, though? She must have wondered surely?" put in Robert.

"Martha never saw the baby until the day she travelled down from Scotland to take charge of him. Then, since her brother claimed the child as his son, there was no reason for her to be suspicious. And naturally, everyone else was ready enough to believe that the fine little boy they saw at the Manor was indeed the Colonel's son. But look at the tea all ready and waiting while I forget my duties!" she laughed as her eye fell on the forgotten tray. "Come along and sit down, all of you. And now, Philippe, perhaps you really will explain just where you have appeared from!"

Chapter 12

PHILIPPE explained the reason for his return and told them all how he had stowed away in his uncle's boat and slept in the cave on Long Holm. But, although it was a fascinating tale, they soon returned to the even more intriguing story that he had unearthed.

"There's still one thing I don't quite see," puzzled Stella. "Why, once the babies had been changed and everyone was satisfied, why did they then have to bother about all this business with the figurehead and *that*?" pointing to the paper that lay beside her father's plate.

"I don't think it's really so hard to understand when you come to think it over," Mr. Bevan answered. "It was natural enough that as time went on the two men should consider the future, and the possible consequences of their action. Colonel Griffiths, in particular, must have wondered how his son would fare when he himself was no longer there to watch over him. He may even have foreseen just such a predicament as that in which poor Sammy finds himself today. It must have been to guard against such a situation that he and his friend worked out this somewhat elaborate plan to safeguard the boy if need be. I suppose they chose the figurehead as their hiding place because it was the only possession the Captain had to leave to the boy. That's why he impressed on Martha the importance of keeping it, although, of course, they meant to include her in the secret eventually."

"Yes, that's just what she said herself," put in Stella.

"One thing is clear," her father went on thoughtfully. "They obviously never intended telling Hubert, otherwise the old man would undoubtedly have left a copy of this declaration among his papers. I suppose he felt there was no need for the boy to know the truth, as long as things continued to run smoothly."

"That's just it!" interrupted Robert. "After all, it's entirely his own fault that things aren't running smoothly for Sammy now."

"Poor Hubert," sighed Mr. Bevan, "I can't help feeling sorry for him all the same. This discovery will be something of a shock to him, I'm afraid."

Stella stole a glance at Philippe, and guessed that he was wondering once again whether the secret would have been better undiscovered. Then, remembering Sammy, she burst out defensively—

"Anyway, however much of a shock it is for him, it couldn't be as bad as poor old Sammy parted from his creatures, and all of them depending on him so. I'm quite sure Colonel Griffiths would have wanted to stop all that unhappiness."

They all looked up at the click of the garden gate and were startled to see Mr. Griffiths himself coming slowly up the path. Mr. Bevan jumped up and hurried out to meet him, bringing him into the room through the french windows.

"You're just in time for a cup of tea," smiled Mrs. Bevan. "Fetch another cup, will you, Stella dear."

"Or would you perhaps prefer something stronger?" suggested the children's father, noting their guest's drawn face.

"No, tea'll be fine, thanks," replied Mr. Griffiths, accepting the cup from Mrs. Bevan. "Well," he added, looking sombrely round on them all, "no doubt these young people have told you the whole extraordinary story?"

"They have," replied Mr. Bevan, "but no one else has heard a word of it, and you can rest assured that the news will never go beyond these four walls; it is your own personal secret and yours it shall remain, as far as we are concerned. I promise you I can trust these youngsters of mine, and I am sure Philippe can be trusted, too."

"Oh, yes, indeed, please!" cried poor Philippe, feeling that he had caused quite enough trouble already.

Mr. Griffith drank his tea before continuing—

"It's a bit of a poser for me as you can guess, and it will need a deal of thinking over, since it appears that I was never adopted legally. Nevertheless, it seems to me that since I have been purposely trained for the position I hold through the connivance of my two fathers, then perhaps it is right for me to carry on with the work they intended me to do."

"I couldn't agree with you more strongly," declared Mr. Bevan emphatically. "And what's more I see absolutely no point in letting anyone else into a secret that those two good men guarded with so much care."

Mr. Griffiths smiled a trifle sadly.

"If I had been as good a man as they were, the secret never need have come out now," he said ruefully. "It was my own ruthlessness in seizing Sammy's cottage that plunged the poor fellow into the predicament from which these young people so rightly planned to rescue him."

Then, turning to Philippe with a quick smile, he went on, "Well, at least you have done what you set out to do; thanks to your intervention, Sammy's future is now assured. The shore cottage and all it contains, inside and out, will be his for the rest of his life. And I also intend putting a sum of money at the disposal of those good neighbours who are already looking after him so well."

"Oh, how kind!" cried Stella joyfully.

"Not really so kind when you think it over," he reminded her quietly. "In point of fact, the cottage—and indeed most of the village—is really his by right already. If you look into it, you will realise that I am really Sammy, son of Captain Walters, with no possessions in the world other than a worm-eaten figurehead and a few hard-luck animals, and the use of the shore cottage for as long as its owner chooses to lend it to me!

"And now, if you will excuse me, Mrs. Bevan, I will go home and put these arrangements for Sammy into writing straightaway; I don't intend there to be any doubt as to his rights to that cottage if he should outlive me. Nor do I intend to entrust these arrangements to a figurehead, there mightn't be anyone as intelligent as young Philippe around when they are needed!" he added smiling, as he made his way out to the garden.

Philippe smiled too, happy to know that, after all, Mr. Griffiths bore him no resentment.

Now at last the family really had time to give their full attention to Philippe's own story, and they persuaded him to tell it right from the beginning again.

"And you mean to say your parents believe you are in Roscoff at this minute?" said Mrs. Bevan doubtfully.

"Yes," said Philippe, "and, please, they must go on believing it, else my father would be very much angry. You will not write? You will not tell them, please?" he finished anxiously, looking from one face to another.

"He'll be home as soon as a letter anyway," put in Stella quickly.

"Well, since you are sailing on the morning tide, I suppose you really will reach Roscoff almost as soon as a letter could do," said Mrs. Bevan. "And, in any case, we will naturally respect your confidence, since we can see for ourselves that you are in no danger and your parents not likely to be worrying. But you're not spending another night on Long Holm! Come, Stella, we'll make up the spare-room bed."

Philippe went into town on the early bus to catch his train next morning, and Stella and her brothers went to the station with him.

Stella was surprised to find that this good-bye was not miserable at all. She and Philippe had done so much since their last good-bye that they were already planning what they would do when she went to stay in Brittany next summer.

"It might be worth looking out for *Michelle* this afternoon," said Philippe as he hung out of the carriage window waiting for the train to start. "Yves says my uncle might call at Tenby on the return trip, and if so, we would pass your part of the coast. So you'd better look out in case."

"How would we recognise her?" asked Robert.

"She is painted brilliant green; you do not seem to have many boats painted in colours like that in your country; *Michelle* was the only one in Barry, anyway."

"We'll be watching," promised Stella. "And if you do come past, look out for our house and imagine us all in the garden waving like mad."

"And imagine me under a pile of fishing nets in the hold!" laughed Philippe. "I'll still be in hiding, you remember, so it will not be possible for me to wave."

He made up for this as the train pulled out, waving until he was carried out of sight around the curve.

"And now for Captain Morgan's," cried Robert, already on his way to the station exit.

"It'll hardly be open yet," Peter reminded him.

This did not stop Robert hurrying through the deserted streets as though the shop might already be crammed with customers queuing to buy the telescope which, thanks to his godfather's parting gift, he could now afford to buy himself. They arrived at the shop as the owner was unlocking the door. They were the only customers and the telescope was still there. Three minutes later Robert walked out of the shop with the precious parcel under his arm.

On the way home in the bus, Peter had a good idea.

"Let's go out in the *Evening Star* after lunch," he suggested. "Then if *Michelle* does come along we'll get a much closer view than we could from the garden."

"Oh, yes, and I'll take my telescope, that'll bring her closer still," said Robert.

Directly lunch was over they set off for the shore. Peter carried the sails and oars and Robert, the rudder and his telescope. Stella brought a bag of small red apples from the garden; there was no knowing how long they might be out and she had noticed that boating made one very hungry.

The sea was glassy calm and they soon pushed the *Evening Star* out beyond the waves which were, in fact, scarcely more than ripples.

"No use attempting to sail in the bay," said Peter regretfully. "There's precious little wind today in any case, and what there is is completely blanketed by the wretched headland.

Once clear of its shelter, though, we should get more breeze. There are plenty of cats' paws on the water farther out."

Stella reached for the rowlocks and dropped them into position. Then Robert got out the oars and began to row. They were a heavy load and it was a long, slow pull out to the ruffled waters beyond the head.

Stella took out an apple and began to eat it in a special way Philippe had taught her, drawing out the juice in slow, rhythmic sucks that sounded exactly like the backwash of waves on a shingle shore. The sound fired her imagination, and closing her eyes, she pictured herself as a castaway on a lone dream island under a swaying palm tree. Robert's voice broke into this delightful vision—

"Must you make that disgusting noise?"

Since the apple was sucked dry anyway, she threw the core into the sea and watched it sink out of sight in the deep green water. Then a breath of freshening wind on her cheek turned her thoughts in a new direction, and, sliding well forward into the bow, she rested her folded arms on the gunwale, picturing herself as a figurehead with the sea wind on her face. But this new dream was shattered, too, this time by Peter.

"Ah, here comes the wind at last!" he exclaimed. "Might as well ship the oars now, Robert, and see if she will sail."

Stella knew that the time had come to abandon dreams and take her place as an alert and useful member of the crew. She slid back from the bow and shrank down into her usual position, out of the way of the sails, yet ready to be called upon to do whatever might be needed. Her first job was to remove the rowlocks and stow them out of the way.

Then she turned and looked ahead to where a dark patch on the water marked the track of an advancing puff of wind.

Next moment it was upon them, and the boat heeled over momentarily as her sails took the strain. Then, righting herself, she began to move steadily across the bay. Away to their right the uneasy current of the Race could just be seen running out to sea. It was quiet today but a danger nonetheless, and Peter gave it a wide berth.

"If *Michelle* does come, how far out d'you suppose she'll be?" asked Robert.

"Well, she's bound to keep outside the buoys," said Peter. "So as long as we keep to the landward side of those, we won't be in her way."

"Anyhow, steam gives way to sail, doesn't it?" observed Stella, glad of a chance to air her nautical knowledge.

"Ye-es," said Peter slowly. "All the same, I'd hate to make a busy ship give way; they'd think us pretty amateur if we did that, you know."

The sun made such a glitter on the water that *Michelle* was already drawing near before they spotted her.

"There she is!" shouted Stella suddenly.

"Oh, surely not," objected Peter, "she's much too big."

"She's not so big when you see her close," declared Robert with his eye to the telescope.

"And she's green," added Stella.

"Maybe you're right," said Peter, "boats do look unnaturally large when seen from water level, I know."

As the boat came nearer, she seemed to shrink in size and soon they were all able to see her bright-green paint.

"There seem to be several people on deck," reported Robert, still glued to the telescope.

"Ready about," called Peter, and he swung the *Evening Star* onto the other tack. She was now travelling down channel with the oncoming boat, but at an angle that would eventually bring them much closer together. They could now hear the steady throb of the engine reverberating over the water. Suddenly they were surprised by another sound, the shrill "peep-peep" of a siren.

"Sounds as though she's calling to us," remarked Stella. "Only she wouldn't be, of course, because only Philippe knows who we are, and he is hiding below. Oh, isn't it thrilling to look at a ship and know that there is a stowaway on board! Look! There they go again! Pete, it must be for us."

"Can't be, surely," said Peter, glancing over his shoulder to see if there was another vessel in sight. But as the *Evening Star* was the only boat to be seen in the whole sweep of sea they came to the conclusion that the greeting must really be meant for them.

"I wish we could reply," said Robert longingly, "but hush, what's she doing now?" He raised his hand to silence any interruption as the siren began to send out a whole series of blasts, some short and sharp, some longer.

"Morse," he breathed. "Sh—let me get it."

They sat in silence until the message came to an end. Then the boys looked at one another questioningly.

"*Evening Star*," said Robert. "At least that's what I thought it was. Was that what you got, Pete?"

"I think so," said Peter. "I lost a bit towards the end but I got 'E-V-E-N-I' quite distinctly."

"And I got 'S-T-A-R' so it must be us," said Robert.

"But I can't understand it," puzzled Peter. "She wouldn't sound her siren without the skipper's orders, and he can't know anything about us."

"Well, those people on deck are waving, anyway," said Stella, raising both her arms in an answering salute.

Michelle gave one more shrill "peep-peep" and then they saw that she was altering course.

"Swinging out to round the second buoy," said Peter.

Suddenly, as Stella watched, one of the figures on deck flung something high into the air. It sailed towards them in a wide arc, glittering momentarily as it splashed into the sea astern. *Michelle*'s attendant gulls swerved aside, swooping down to examine the object before returning to their positions in the wake of the little green vessel.

"We'll have to be turning back ourselves," said Peter. "Ready abou . . ."

"Oh, Peter, wait!" shrilled Stella. "We must go and see what they threw us. I'm keeping my eyes fixed on the spot where it fell."

"Oh, we must get back," said Peter impatiently. "We're a long way out and it's getting late. Anyway, that wouldn't be anything to do with us, just some rubbish out of the galley, I expect."

"But it sparkled in the sun, and it hasn't sunk, I can still see it. Oh, Peter, please, let's just go and look at it in case," pleaded Stella.

"Oh, all right," grumbled Peter with a noticeable lack of enthusiasm, "where is it anyway? Ah, yes, I see. O.K., then, I'll pass to windward of it, and if it looks worth picking up, one of you'd better grab it as we go by."

"It's a float, one of the aluminum kind," reported Robert as they drew near.

"Get ready to pull it in, then," ordered Peter. "I'll pass as close to it as I can."

They were so intent on the job that they almost missed the final glimpse of *Michelle,* but she gave one last "peep" on her siren and they turned, just in time to see her vanishing round the headland in a flurry of following gulls.

"Now," said Peter, "I'll keep her as she is; we should pass close enough to reach it. You try first Stella, only don't fall in whatever you do, no float is worth that. Besides, if you miss, Robert should be able to get it."

Stella gritted her teeth, determined not to miss. A moment later she had the dripping float in her lap.

"There's a little bottle tied to it!" she cried excitedly. "That must have been what I saw sparkling. Oh, and there's something inside the bottle, too—a bit of paper folded very small. I bet it's a message!"

"Let's see," said Robert, holding out his hand. But Stella clung to her prize determined to open it herself. The screw top was very difficult to undo, but ignoring Robert's offers of help she worked it loose and pulled out a grubby sheet of paper smelling powerfully of onions. Its message was written in blunted pencil.

"It's from Philippe!" she exclaimed, catching sight of the signature.

"Here, let's see!" demanded Robert, reaching for it again.

But Stella dodged back under the sail and from this secure position read the pencilled message aloud:

" 'To *Evening Star* from *Michelle*. Oncle Jacques has made me a member of his crew for the rest of the holidays, with pay and everything. He was not very angry when he discovered me. *Michelle* will be bringing another load of onions into the Bristol Channel next week. So look out for an "onion johnnie" at the back door! Philippe.' "

She looked up from the paper with shining eyes.

"I shall collect some laverbread ready for his supper when he comes," she decided.

"We'll get Mum to buy all the onions he has left so that he'll be able to spend the rest of his time ashore with us," said Robert.

"He might even have time to come out for a sail," said Peter. "Now then, ready about."

As the little boat sped in towards the shore Stella slid under the foresail and crawled to her favourite position in the bow. As the wind caressed her cheek she felt herself a figurehead again. And how right it seemed that she, with her own star name, should act as figurehead to a boat named *Evening Star*.

Her gaze turned towards the shore cottage. Something could just be seen moving about in front of it. She knew this must be Sammy, pottering happily about the home he had so nearly lost, and although she could not see them, she could picture the creatures that were undoubtedly accompanying him. Above him she could just make out the motionless form of the figurehead. She knew the painted eyes would be turned in her direction, and a little wordless greeting went winging over the water to the shorebound, wooden *Evelyn Starr* from the happy, living figurehead in the bow of the *Evening Star*.

Rosalie Fry

ROSALIE FRY'S love of country life and travel is reflected in the books she has written and illustrated for children.

Miss Fry was born on Vancouver Island, Canada, and has traveled extensively throughout Europe. During World War II she was stationed in the Orkney Islands, where she coded and decoded messages as a Cypher officer in the Women's Royal Naval Service. She now lives in Swansea, South Wales.

Florence, Venice and Assisi are the scenes of *Fly Home, Colombina. The Mountain Door* takes place in Ireland, *The Echo Song* is set in Wales, and *Secret of the Ron Mor Skerry* in the Western Isles off the coast of Scotland. Among Miss Fry's other books for young people are *Matelot, Little Sailor of Brittany* and *A Bell for Ringelblume.*